Rebecca of
Sunnybrook Farm

Rebecca of Sunnybrook Farm

by KATE DOUGLAS WIGGIN

Edited and Abridged
by Gladys P. Schwarcz

Illustrated by Ethel Gold

SCHOLASTIC INC.
New York Toronto London Auckland Sydney

ISBN 0-590-04487-7

12 11 10 9 8 7   5 6 7 8 9/8   0/9

Printed in the U.S.A.   01

To my mother

Contents

We Are Seven

THE OLD STAGECOACH was rumbling along the dusty Maine road that runs from Maplewood to Riverboro. It was a warm day — warm as midsummer though it was only the middle of May — and the driver was letting the horses amble at their own pace.

There was one small passenger in the coach — a slender, dark-haired girl. Her cotton dress was so stiffly starched that she jounced and slid from side to side on the leather cushions whenever the wheels jolted over a rut in the road.

Early that morning, as the driver was about to leave the post office in Maplewood, a woman had asked him if this was the Riverboro stage and if he was the driver, Mr. Cobb. When he said yes, she nodded to a young girl who ran forward eagerly. The woman helped her up into the stagecoach and placed a small bundle and a bouquet of lilacs beside her. Then the woman checked to see that Mr. Cobb roped an old hair trunk firmly onto the back of the stagecoach. Finally, as she carefully counted out the fare, the woman said, "I want you to take my daughter to my sisters in Riverboro. Do you know Mirandy and Jane Sawyer? They live in the brick house."

Mr. Cobb nodded.

"Well, that's where she's going, and they're expecting her. Will you keep an eye on her, please?" The woman spoke into the coach: "Good-bye, Rebecca. Try not to get into any mischief, and sit quiet so you'll look neat and nice when you get there. Don't be any trouble to Mr. Cobb."

"Good-bye, Mother, don't worry. It isn't as if I hadn't traveled before."

The woman gave a little laugh. "She's been to Wareham and stayed overnight," she said to Mr. Cobb. "That isn't much to be journey-proud on!"

"It *was traveling*, Mother," said the girl. "It was leaving the farm, and putting up lunch in a basket, and taking the train, and carrying our nightgowns — "

"Don't tell the whole village about it, if we did," said her mother, interrupting her. "Haven't I told you before that you shouldn't talk about nightgowns and things like that in a loud tone of voice, and especially when there's menfolks around?"

"I know, Mother, I know, and I won't. All I want to say is —" at that moment Mr. Cobb gave a cluck to the horses, slapped the reins, and the stage was under way. Rebecca had to put her head out of the window of the door in order to finish her sentence " — it *is* a journey when you carry a nightgown!"

The words floated back. Mrs. Randall shaded her eyes with her hand and watched the stage out of sight.

"Mirandy'll have her hands full," she said to herself, "but it should be the making of Rebecca."

Before a half hour had passed, the sun, the heat, and the dust had relaxed Mr. Cobb so completely that he had forgotten his promise to keep an eye on Rebecca.

Suddenly he heard a small voice above the rattle of the wheels and turned to look over his shoulder. He saw a small shape hanging out the window and a long black braid of hair swinging with the motion of the coach as his passenger made feeble attempts to poke him with her pink sunshade.

"Please let me speak!" Rebecca called.

Mr. Cobb drew up the horses.

"Does it cost any more to ride up there with you?" she asked. "It's so slippery down here that I rattle around. I'm almost black and blue, and the windows are so small I can only see pieces of things. I've almost broken my neck stretching around to find out whether my trunk has fallen off the back. It's my mother's trunk, and she's very fond of it."

Mr. Cobb waited until this flood of criticism had ended, then said, "You can come up if you want to. There ain't no extra charge to sit side of me." With that he climbed down, helped her out of the stage, boosted her up to the front seat, and got back in his own place.

Rebecca sat down carefully, smoothing her dress beneath her. She put her sunshade on the seat between Mr. Cobb and herself, and covered it with the edge of her skirt. Then she pushed back her hat, pulled up her darned white cotton gloves, and said delightedly, "Oh! this is better! This is like traveling! I hope we have a long, long way to go?"

"We've only just started," Mr. Cobb replied. "It takes more than two hours."

"Only two hours," she sighed. "I brought some lunch with me because Mother said it would be a bad beginning to get to the brick house hungry and have Aunt Mirandy get me something to eat the first thing. . . . It's a good *growing* day, isn't it?"

"It certainly is, but too hot. Why don't you put up your parasol?"

Rebecca pulled the edge of her dress still farther over the sunshade. "Oh dear no! I never put it up when the sun shines. Pink fades awfully, you know, and I only carry it to church on cloudy Sundays. Sometimes the sun comes out all of a sudden and I have a dreadful time covering it up. It's the dearest thing in life to me, but it's an awful worry."

It slowly dawned on Jeremiah Cobb that his young passenger was quite a different person from those he usually carried. He pushed his hat back and took his first good look at Rebecca — a look which she met with a stare of friendly curiosity.

Mr. Cobb observed that her cotton dress was faded, but spotlessly clean and starched. Her dark hair under her straw hat hung to her waist in a thick braid, and her small, sharp face was pale. But it was her eyes that particularly caught Mr. Cobb's attention. They were like two stars, full of dancing

13

lights, and they glanced about with eager interest.

"Miss Ross, a lady who paints, gave me the sunshade," Rebecca said, when she had exchanged looks with Mr. Cobb and learned his face by heart. "The handle is scarred, you see. That's because Fanny chewed on it in church when I wasn't looking. I've never felt the same about Fanny since."

"Is Fanny your sister?"

"She's one of them."

"How many of you are there?"

"Seven. Hannah is the oldest. I come next, then John, then Jenny, then Mark, then Fanny, then Mira."

"Well, that *is* a big family!"

"Far too big, everybody says." Such frankness caused Mr. Cobb to murmur, "I swan!"

"They're dear, but such a bother. And they cost so much to feed," she continued. "Hannah and I haven't done anything for years and years but put babies to bed at night and take them up in the morning. But it's finished, that's one comfort, and we'll have a lovely time when we're all grown up and the mortgage is paid off."

"All finished? Oh, you mean now that you've come away?"

"No, I mean our family's finished. Mira,

she's three, was born the day Father died. Aunt Miranda wanted Hannah to come to Riverboro instead of me, but Mother couldn't spare her. She takes hold of housework better than I do, and Mother has the cooking and the farm too."

"Oh, you live on a farm, do ye? Where is it? Near where you got on?"

"Near? No, it must be thousands of miles away! We took the train from Temperance. Then we drove a long way to Cousin Ann's and went to bed. Then we got up and drove ever so far to Maplewood to meet you. Our farm is away off from everything, but our school and church are only two miles away in Temperance."

"I've been to Temperance — used to live up that way — but I can't seem to locate your farm. What's your folks' name?"

"Randall. My mother's name is Aurelia Randall. Our names are Hannah Lucy Randall, Rebecca Rowena Randall, John Halifax Randall, Jenny Lind Randall, Marquis Randall, Fanny Ellsler Randall, and Miranda Randall. Mother named half of us and Father the other half, but we didn't come out even, so they both thought it would be nice to name Mira after Aunt Miranda in Riverboro. They hoped it might do some good, but it didn't.

"We are all named after somebody in particular. Hannah and John and I were all named after people in books. My name was taken out of *Ivanhoe*. Mark is named after Father's dead twin brother, Marquis de Lafayette. We don't call him Marquis, only Mark. Jenny is named for a singer and Fanny for a beautiful dancer, but Mother says they're both misfits, for Jenny can't carry a tune and Fanny's kind of stiff-legged. Mother would like to call them Jane and Frances and give up their middle names, but she says it wouldn't be fair to Father. She says we must always stand up for Father because everything was against him and he wouldn't have died if he hadn't had such bad luck. I think that's all there is to tell about us."

"Land of Liberty! I should think it was enough," exclaimed Mr. Cobb. "You've got a powerful good memory! I guess it ain't no trouble for you to learn your lessons, is it?"

"Not much. The trouble is to get the shoes to go to them. These are new ones I've got on and they have to last six months. There don't seem to be any way of saving shoes except taking them off and going barefoot. But I can't do that in Riverboro without shaming Aunt Mirandy. I'm going to school while I live with Aunt Mirandy, and then in two years I'm going on to the academy at Wareham. I'm going to be a painter like Miss Ross when I get through school. At any rate, that's what *I* think I'm going to be. Mother thinks I'd better teach."

"Your farm ain't the old Hobbs place, is it?" Mr. Cobb was still trying to place Rebecca's home.

"No, it's just Randall's Farm. At least that's what Mother calls it. I call it Sunnybrook Farm."

"I guess it don't make no difference what you call it so long as you know where it is," Mr. Cobb remarked.

Rebecca turned her eyes full on him. "Oh, don't say that. It does make a difference what you call things. When I say Randall's Farm, do you see how it looks?"

"No, I can't say I do," Mr. Cobb replied uneasily.

"Now when I say Sunnybrook Farm, what does it make you think of?"

Mr. Cobb felt helpless. There was no avoiding a reply, for Rebecca's eyes were like searchlights piercing his brain

"I suppose there's a brook somewhere near it," he said timidly.

Rebecca looked disappointed but not disheartened. "That's pretty good," she said. "You're warm but not hot. There's a brook, but not a common brook. It has trees and bushes on each side of it, and a white sandy bottom with lots of little shiny pebbles. Whenever there's a bit of sunshine, the brook catches it."

Rebecca was quiet for a while. When she spoke again it was on an entirely new subject. "Don't your stomach feel hollow?" she asked. "Mine does! I was so afraid I'd miss the stage I couldn't eat any breakfast."

"You'd better have your lunch then," Mr. Cobb suggested. "I don't eat till I get to Milltown."

"I wish I could see Milltown. I suppose it's bigger and grander even than Wareham — more like Paris? Miss Ross told me about Paris. She bought my pink sunshade there, and my bead purse."

"Paris ain't so great," said Mr. Cobb. "It's the dullest place in the state of Maine. I've been there many a time."

Rebecca felt obliged to correct Mr. Cobb. "Paris is the capital of France. You have to go to it on a boat. It's in my geography. But *you* can see Milltown most every day," Rebecca added wistfully.

"Milltown ain't so great, neither," replied Mr. Cobb, with the air of having visited all the cities of the earth and found them lacking. "If your Aunt Mirandy'll let you, I'll take you down to Milltown some day this summer when the stage ain't full."

"You will!" A thrill of excitement ran through Rebecca. "It's just like having a fairy godmother give you your wish. Did you ever read 'Cinderella' or 'The Yellow Dwarf' or 'The Enchanted Frog' or 'The Fair One with Golden Locks'?"

"No," said Mr. Cobb, after a moment's thought. "I never did."

"I've read lots of books," Rebecca said. "Father's and Miss Ross's and my school-teachers', and all those in the Sunday-school library. I've read *The Lamplighter* and *Scottish Chiefs* and *Ivanhoe* and *David Copperfield* and *Plutarch's Lives* and *Pilgrim's Progress* and —"

Pointing into the distance, Mr. Cobb interrupted Rebecca's recital. "There's the river," he said. "This is the last long hill. When we get to the top of it, we'll see the chimneys of Riverboro in the distance. It ain't far. I live about half a mile from the brick house — across the river."

Rebecca stirred nervously. "I didn't think I

was going to be afraid," she said. "But I guess I am, now you say it's coming so near."

"Want to go back?" asked Mr. Cobb curiously.

"No," she said proudly. "I might be frightened, but I'd be ashamed to run." She flashed him a courageous look. "Is there a main street to the village, like there is in Wareham?"

"I suppose you might call it a main street. Your Aunts Sawyer live on it, but there ain't no stores nor mills. It's a one-horse village! You have to cross the river to our side if you want to see anything going on."

"I'm kind of sorry," Rebecca sighed. "It would be grand to drive down a real main street, sitting high up like this behind two splendid horses, with my pink sunshade up and everybody in town wondering who the hair trunk belongs to."

"There ain't no harm, as I can see, in our making a grand entry," Mr. Cobb said. "I'll take the whip out, sit up straight, and drive fast. You sit up straight, and open your parasol. We'll just make everybody stare!"

Rebecca's face was radiant, but the glow faded quickly. "I forgot — Mother put me inside. She'd want me to be there when I got to Aunt Mirandy's. Maybe it would be better if I sat inside. Then I wouldn't have to jump down and my clothes wouldn't fly up. Instead I could open the door and step down like a lady. Would you please stop a minute, Mr. Cobb, and let me change places?"

The good-natured stage driver pulled up the horses, lifted Rebecca down, and helped her inside the coach.

"We've had a great trip," he said, "and we've got real well acquainted, haven't we? You won't forget about Milltown?"

"Never!" she exclaimed with great spirit. "And you're sure you won't either?"

"Never. Cross my heart!" Mr. Cobb vowed solemnly, as he climbed back to his seat.

A few minutes later, when the stage turned into the yard beside the old brick house, Mrs. Perkins, the Sawyers' next door neighbor, saw a proper young lady sitting primly in the back seat.

Rebecca's journey had ended.

A Difference in Hearts

*I*T HAD BEEN several years since Miranda and Jane Sawyer had seen the Randall children, but they had never forgotten them. Hannah, the eldest, had not spoken a word during that visit. It was for this reason that they later invited her to come to Riverboro to become a member of their family.

They suffered rather a shock then when they received their sister's letter telling them that Hannah could not be spared, but that Rebecca would come as soon as she could be made ready. The memory of Rebecca was still painfully vivid to Miranda and Jane. Their sister, however, was most thankfully appreciative of their offer, and added that the regular schooling and church privileges, as well as the influence of the Sawyer home, would doubtless be "the making of Rebecca."

"I don't know as I calculated to be the making of any child," Miranda had said when Aurelia's letter arrived. "I thought Aurelia would send us the one we asked for, but it's just like her to palm off that wild young one on somebody else."

"We said that Rebecca or even Jenny might come if Hannah couldn't," Jane reminded her.

"I know we did, but we hadn't any notion it would turn out that way," grumbled Miranda.

"Rebecca was a mite of a thing when we saw her three years ago," ventured Jane. "She's had time to improve."

"And time to grow worse!"

"Won't it be kind of a privilege to put her on the right track?" Jane asked timidly.

"I don't know about the privilege part, but it'll be a big chore. If her mother ain't got her on the right track by now, she won't take to it herself all of a sudden."

Miranda's depressing frame of mind lasted until the day and the hour that Mr. Cobb and his coach were due to arrive with Rebecca.

"The stage ought to be here," said Miranda, glancing nervously at the tall clock for the twentieth time. "I guess everything's done. We've baked and scrubbed and cleaned, but children are awful hard on a house. I expect we shan't know it a year from now."

Jane's spirit had naturally been affected by Miranda's gloom. But there was a basic difference in thinking and feeling between the sisters in this matter. While Miranda wondered how they could endure Rebecca, Jane wondered at times how Rebecca would endure them! It was during one of these times that she ran upstairs to Rebecca's room to put a vase of apple blossoms and a red pincushion on her bureau.

The stage rumbled up to the side door of the brick house, and Mr. Cobb handed Rebecca out like a real lady passenger. She stepped down carefully, put the bunch of faded lilacs in Aunt Miranda's hand, and received a hasty kiss.

"You needn't have bothered to bring flowers," said Miranda with her usual lack of tact. "The garden's always full of 'em."

Jane kissed Rebecca with more warmth, then she turned to Mr. Cobb and said, "Put the trunk in the entry, Jeremiah, and we'll get it carried upstairs this afternoon."

"Well, good-bye, Rebecca," Mr. Cobb said. "Good-day, Mirandy — Jane. You've got a lively little girl there. She'll be first-rate company."

Miranda Sawyer shuddered. She believed that children might be seen, if absolutely necessary, but they certainly should never be heard.

"We're not much used to noise," she remarked acidly.

Mr. Cobb saw that he had taken the wrong tack, but he was not used to argument so he said nothing. As he drove away he tried to think of a word other than lively with which he might have safely described his young passenger.

"I'll take you up and show you your room, Rebecca," Aunt Miranda said. "Shut the screen door tight behind you, so's to keep the flies out. It ain't flytime yet, but I want you to start right. Rub your feet on that braided rug and hang your hat in the entry there as you go past."

"It's my best hat," said Rebecca.

"Take it upstairs then and put it in the clothes closet, but I shouldn't have thought you'd wear your best hat on the stage."

"It's my only hat," explained Rebecca. "My everyday hat wasn't good enough to bring. Fanny's going to have it."

"Lay your parasol in the entry closet."

"Do you mind if I keep it in my room, please? It always seems safer."

"There ain't any thieves hereabouts, and if there was, I guess they wouldn't make for your sunshade. Come along. Remember to always use the back way. We don't use the front stairs on account of the carpet. Take care of the turn and don't catch your foot. Here's your room on the right. When you've washed your face and hands and brushed your hair, come down. We'll unpack your trunk later and get you settled before supper. Ain't you got your dress on backwards?"

Rebecca drew her chin down and looked at the row of smoked pearl buttons running up and down the middle of her chest.

"Backwards? Oh, I see! No, it's on right. Mother always says, if you have seven children you can't keep buttoning and unbuttoning 'em all the time — they have to do it for themselves. Dresses always button in the front at our house."

Miranda said nothing but she closed the door of the room firmly.

Rebecca stood perfectly still in the center of the floor and looked about her. There was a square of linoleum in front of each piece of furniture and a hooked rug beside the single four-poster bed, which was covered with a fringed white cotton spread.

Everything was very neat, but the ceilings were much higher than Rebecca was used to. The room faced north, and the long, narrow window looked out on the back buildings and the barn.

It was not the strange room, or the long journey, or the fear of her grim aunt that made Rebecca suddenly act as she did — it was the combination of everything. She stood her sunshade in the corner, tore off her hat and flung it on the bureau, stripped down the spread, and jumped into the middle of the bed. Then she pulled the spread over her head.

In a moment the door opened quietly, and Aunt Miranda entered. Her eyes wandered about the vacant room, then fell upon the heaving bedspread.

"Rebecca!"

The word might have been shouted from the housetops.

A dark ruffled head and two frightened eyes appeared above the spread.

"Why are you lying on your good bed in the daytime — messing and dirtying it up with your dusty boots?"

Rebecca rose guiltily. "I'm sorry, Aunt Mirandy. Something came over me. I don't know what."

"Well, if it comes over you very soon again we'll have to find out what it is. Smooth your bed this minute. Abijah Flagg's bringing your trunk upstairs, and I wouldn't let him see such a cluttered-up room for anything. He'd tell it all over town."

That night Jeremiah Cobb tried to describe Rebecca to his wife, but he couldn't seem to find the right words. Finally, he gave up and said, "She'll be coming over to see you, Sarah, and you can size her up for yourself. But I don't know how she'll get on with Mirandy Sawyer — poor little soul!"

Rebecca's first letters to her mother indicated that getting along with Aunt Miranda was going to be far from easy.

Dear Mother — I am safely here. My dress was not much tumbled and Aunt Jane helped me press it out. I like Mr. Cobb very much. I rode outside a little while, but got inside before I got to Aunt Miranda's house. I did not want to, but thought you would like it better. Miranda is such a long word that I will say Aunt M. and Aunt J. in my

Sunday letters. Aunt J. has given me a dictionary to look up the spelling of all the hard words. It takes a good deal of time and I don't always use it. I am glad people can talk without stopping to spell. It is much easier to talk than write, and much more fun. The brick house looks just the way you told us. The parlor is splendid and gives you creeps and chills when you look in the door. The furnature is ellergant too, but there are no good sitting-down places except in the kitchen. The same cat is here but they do not save kittens when she has them, and the cat is too old to play with. Hannah told me once that you ran away from here with Father. I can see it would be nice. If Aunt M. would run away I think I should like to live with Aunt J. She does not hate me as bad as Aunt M. does. Tell Mark he can have my paint box, but I should like him to save some of the red paint in case I come home again. I hope Hannah and John do not get tired doing my chores.

Your afectionate friend,
Rebecca

P.S. Please give the piece of poetry to

John because he likes my poetry even
when it is not very good. This piece is
not very good, but it is true. I hope
you won't mind what is in it, as you
ran away.

SUNDAY THOUGHTS

By

Rebecca Rowena Randall

This house is dark and dull and drear
No light doth shine from far or near
Nor ever could.

And those of us who live here herein
Are most as dead as seraphim
Though not as good.

My guardian angel is asleep
At least he doth no vigil keep
But far doth roam.

Then give me back my lonely farm
Where none alive did wish me harm,
Dear childhood home!

Dear Mother — I am thrilling with
unhappiness this morning. I got that
out of a book. Aunt M. is very cross
and unfealing to me. I wish Hannah

had come instead of me. It was Hannah that was wanted and she is better than I am and does not answer back so quick. Are there any peaces left of my buff calico? Aunt J. wants enough to make a new waist for my dress that will button in the back, so I wont look so outlandish. The styles are quite pretty in Riverboro and those at church quite ellergant, more so than in Temperance.

Your affectionate friend,
Rebecca

Dear Mother — School is pretty good. The teacher can answer more questions than the Temperance one, but not so many as I can ask. I am smarter than all the girls but one, but not so smart as two boys. Emma Jane Perkins, who lives next door, can add and subtract in her head like a streek of lightning and knows the speling book right through, but has no thoughts of any kind. She is in the Third Reader but does not like stories in books. I am in the Sixth Reader but because I cannot say the seven multiplication table Miss Dearborn threttens to put me in the baby class with Elijah and Elisha Simpson, little twins.

I am going to try for the speling prize but fear I cannot get it. I would not care but wrong speling looks dreadful in poetry.

I am glad our cow has a calf and it is spotted. It is going to be a good year for apples and hay so you and John will be glad and we can pay a little more morgage. Miss Dearborn asked us what is the object of edducation and I said the object of mine was to help pay off the morgage. She told Aunt M. and I had to sew extra for punishment because she says a morgage is a disgrace like stealing or smallpox and it will be all over town that we have one on our farm. Emma Jane is not morgaged nor Richard Carter nor Dr. Winship, but the Simpsons are.

Your loving little friend,
Rebecca

Wisdom's Ways

On THE MONDAY AFTER her arrival in Riverboro, Rebecca began her education. The school was in Riverboro Center, about a mile distant, so Miranda Sawyer borrowed a neighbor's horse and wagon and drove her niece to school the first moring. She interviewed the teacher, Miss Dearborn, arranged for books, and generally saw to it that Rebecca started on the right path to knowledge.

Every day after that Rebecca walked to school. When the weather was fair, she took a shortcut. She would leave the main road and cross a pasture, waving away the cows, race down a little hill, and jump from stone to stone across a woodland brook. How delicious it was, she would think, and happily swing her lunch pail that contained two crackers spread with butter and syrup, one baked custard, and a square of gingerbread.

Sometimes she would practice whatever poem she was going to recite on the next Friday afternoon. When Emma Jane Perkins took the shortcut with her, they had great fun acting out the dramatic parts of poems.

At the end of the shortcut, the girls sometimes met the Simpson children. Rebecca had felt a great interest in them from the first. There were so many, and they were so patched and darned, that they reminded her of her own family at Sunnybrook.

The little schoolhouse stood on the crest of a hill. There was a flagpole on the roof and two doors in front, one for boys and the other for girls. On one side of the small building stretched rolling fields and meadows; on the other, a pine woods, and the river glinted and sparkled in the distance.

The inside of the schoolhouse was bare and ugly and uncomfortable. This was because the villages along the river spent so much money repairing and rebuilding bridges that they had little left for the school. The teacher's desk and chair stood on a platform. There was an old, sooty stove, a map of the United States, two blackboards, a ten-quart tin pail of water with a long-handled dipper tied to it, and wooden desks and benches for the pupils — twenty of them while Rebecca was in school there.

The more advanced and longer-legged pupils sat in the back of the room on higher seats. They were the envy of their classmates because they were nearer the windows and farther from the teacher.

There were classes of a sort, although few of the pupils studied together from the same book because few were at the same level of learning in any one subject. Rebecca was so difficult to classify that at the end of two weeks Miss Dearborn gave up the attempt altogether. Rebecca did reading with Dick Carter and Living Perkins, who were preparing to enter the academy at Wareham; worked arithmetic with little Susan Simpson; and studied geography with Emma Jane Perkins. She had to practice grammar with Miss Dearborn after school hours, because she was so poor in composition; the work of spelling and punctuation interfered with the free expression of her ideas.

She took history with Alice Robinson's class. Rebecca was told to begin with the discovery of America. In a week she had covered the events up to the Revolution, and in ten days had arrived at Yorktown with the rest of the class. Then she realized that extra effort would mean that she would have to recite with the oldest Simpson boy, so she deliberately held herself back.

Samuel Simpson was called "Seesaw," because he had difficulty in making up his mind. He was further handicapped by a stammer when he became nervous. Perhaps it was because of these weaknesses that Rebecca's decision of character had a fascination for him. Although she snubbed him, he could never keep his eyes away from her. The force with which she tied a shoelace; the way she tossed her braid over her shoulder; her manner of studying — book on desk, arms folded, eyes fixed on the opposite wall — everything she did had charm for Seesaw Simpson. When she walked to the water pail in the corner and drank from the dipper, unseen forces dragged Seesaw from his seat to go and drink after her. He felt a fearful joy in standing next to her, or passing her on the way, even when she gave him a cold, disdainful look.

One warm day in summer, Rebecca was more than usually thirsty. The third time she asked for permission to get a drink, Miss Dearborn nodded yes, but lifted her eyebrows in annoyance. As Rebecca replaced the dipper, Seesaw promptly raised his hand and Miss Dearborn nodded her head wearily.

"What is the matter with you, Rebecca?" she asked.

"I had salt mackerel for breakfast," Rebecca answered.

There was nothing funny about her reply, for she was merely stating a fact, but an uncontrollable titter ran through the school. Miss Dearborn did not enjoy jokes that she had not made herself. Her face flushed as she said, "I think you had better stand by the pail, Rebecca. It may help you to control your thirst."

Rebecca's heart fluttered. She hated to stand in the corner by the water pail and be stared at by her schoolmates. Unconsciously she made an angry gesture and moved a step nearer her seat, but she was stopped by Miss Dearborn's command: "Stand by the pail, Rebecca! Samuel, how many times have you asked for water today?"

"This is the f-f-fourth."

"Don't touch the dipper, please. The school has done nothing but drink this whole day. It has had no time whatever to study. I suppose you too had something salty for breakfast, Samuel?"

"I had m-m-mackerel, j-just like Reb-b-becca." There were more giggles in the school.

"I judged so. Stand by the other side of the pail, Samuel."

Rebecca's head drooped with shame and anger. Standing in front of the class was bad enough, but to be punished with Seesaw Simpson was beyond human endurance.

Singing was the last exercise in the afternoon. As the class sang, Miss Dearborn stole a look at Rebecca's bent head, and became frightened. Rebecca's face was pale, except for two red spots glowing on her cheeks. Tears hung on her lashes, her breath came and went quickly, and her hands trembled.

"You may go to your seat, Rebecca," Miss Dearborn said at the end of the first song. "Samuel, stay where you are till the close of school. Now class, every time Rebecca has asked for a drink today the whole school has gone to the pail one after another. She is really thirsty, and I daresay I ought to have punished you for following her example, not her for setting it."

Rebecca sank into her seat and pulled the singing book from her desk. Miss Dearborn's public explanation had lifted some of the weight from her heart and she felt better about herself.

Under cover of the singing, Rebecca began to receive signs of sympathy from her classmates. Living Perkins dropped a piece of maple sugar in her lap as he passed her on his way to the blackboard. Alice Robinson rolled a perfectly new slate pencil over the floor with her foot until it reached Rebecca's desk, and her seatmate, Emma Jane, had made up a little round of paper balls and labeled them "Bullets for you know who."

By the time she was alone with her teacher for her grammar lesson, Rebecca had almost recovered her calm, but Miss Dearborn was still disturbed.

"Rebecca, I am afraid I punished you more than I meant to," said Miss Dearborn, who was young and had never seen a child like Rebecca in her one year of teaching.

"I didn't miss a question this whole day, or whisper either," Rebecca said in a quavering voice. "I don't think I ought to be shamed just for drinking."

"You started all the others, or it seemed as if you did. Whatever you do, they all do — whether you laugh, or write notes, or ask to leave the room, or get a drink of water — and it must be stopped."

"Sam Simpson is a copycat!" stormed Rebecca. "I wouldn't have minded standing alone — that is, not so very much — but I couldn't bear standing with him."

"I saw, and that's the reason I told you to take your seat. You must remember that you are a stranger here and the children take more notice of what you do. Now give me some examples of the subjunctive mood, and that will do for our grammar lesson this afternoon."

"If I had not loved mackerel," said Rebecca, "I should not have been thirsty."

Miss Dearborn smiled at her pupil's joke, and when the lesson ended, the two parted good friends.

Sunshine in a Shady Place

*I*T WAS FORTUNATE that Rebecca had her books and her new friends to keep her busy that first summer in Riverboro, or life would have gone heavily for her. The trouble was Aunt Miranda. No matter how hard she tried, Rebecca could not like her aunt. And she felt uncomfortable living under her aunt's roof, eating her food, wearing the clothes and studying the books her aunt provided, while all the time she disliked her relative so heartily. Rebecca felt it was wrong and mean. When she was feeling particularly guilty about it, she made a desperate effort to please her aunt.

But needless to say, Rebecca irritated Miranda with every breath she drew. She continually forgot, and started to go up the front stairs because it was the shortest route to her bedroom. She left the dipper on the kitchen shelf instead of hanging it up over the pail. She went willingly on errands, but often forgot what she was sent out to get. Her tongue was always in motion, either talking, singing, or whistling, and she was always putting flowers in vases, pinning them on her dress, or sticking them in her hat.

Finally, she was a constant reminder of her father, whose handsome face and engaging manner, Miranda felt, had deceived Rebecca's mother. Miranda often compared Rebecca to Hannah. It seemed to her that Hannah took after the Sawyer side of the family, and she couldn't help wishing again and again that the older girl had been the one to become a member of her household.

To Rebecca, Aunt Jane was like finding sunshine in a shady place. During those first difficult weeks, her quiet voice, her understanding look, her ready excuses helped her impulsive little niece settle down into the "brick house ways." By degrees, Rebecca did learn the new ways, but fitting herself to them seemed to make her older than her years.

Every afternoon she took her sewing and sat beside Aunt Jane in the kitchen or worked with her on the side porch, where the clematis and woodbine shaded them from the hot sun. To Rebecca the lengths of brown gingham material were endless. She broke her thread, dropped her thimble, pricked her finger, could not match the checks, and puckered the seams. Still, Aunt Jane was patient.

When the first brown gingham dress was finished, Rebecca asked Aunt Miranda if she might have a brighter color for her next one.

"I bought enough of the brown," Miranda said, "to give you two more dresses, with plenty left over to replace sleeves and to patch and let down hems. It's more economical."

"I know. But Mr. Watson says he'll take back part of it, and let us have some pink and some blue for the same price."

"Did you ask him?"

"Yes'm."

"It was not your business."

"I was helping Emma Jane choose aprons, and didn't think you'd mind which color I had. Pink keeps clean just as nice as brown, and Mr. Watson says it'll boil without fading."

"Mr. Watson's a splendid judge of washing, I suppose. I don't approve of children being rigged out in fancy colors, but I'll see what your Aunt Jane thinks."

"I think it would be all right to let Rebecca have one pink and one blue gingham," said

Jane. "A child gets tired of sewing on one color. It's only natural she should long for a change. Besides, she'd look like a charity child always wearing the same brown."

So finally there was pink gingham. When the dress was finished, Aunt Jane showed Rebecca how to make a pretty trimming of narrow, white linen tape.

"It'll be good handwork for you, Rebecca, for your Aunt Miranda won't like to see you always reading in the long winter evenings. Now if you can baste two rows of white tape around the bottom of your pink skirt, I'll stitch them on for you and trim the waist and sleeves so the dress'll be real pretty for second best."

"I'll baste like a house afire!" Rebecca exclaimed. "It's a thousand yards around that skirt, but I'd sew trimming on it if it was from here to Milltown. Do you think Aunt Mirandy'll ever let me go to Milltown with Mr. Cobb? He's asked me again, you know; but one Saturday I had to pick strawberries, and another it rained. I don't think she really approves of my going."

Without giving her aunt a chance to reply, Rebecca rushed on. "It's *twenty-nine* minutes past four, Aunt Jane, and Alice Robinson has been sitting under the currant bushes for a long time waiting for me. Can I go and play?"

"Yes, you may go. I can see Susan Simpson and the twins and Emma Jane Perkins hiding behind the fence. You'd better go play out behind the barn so's your noise won't distract your Aunt Mirandy."

Rebecca leaped off the porch and pulled Alice Robinson from under the currant bushes. Then by a complicated system of signals to Emma Jane the three older girls managed to give the Simpson children the slip. They were much too small to take part in the activities the girls had planned for that afternoon.

In the Sawyer pasture there was a velvety stretch of ground which the children called the "secret spot." It was full of fascinating hollows and hills, as well as grassy levels. A group of trees concealed it from view. Here, in soap boxes hidden among the trees, the girls stored all their treasures. There were baskets and plates and cups made of burdock burrs; bits of broken china for parties; dolls for acting out characters in all sorts of dramas — deaths, funerals, weddings, and christenings.

On this particular afternoon, a tall, square

house of sticks was to be built around Rebecca. She was to play Charlotte Corday, a woman imprisoned during the French Revolution.

As the other two girls worked, Rebecca stood inside the building with Emma Jane's apron wound about her hair. When she leaned her head against the sticks, they became cold iron bars, and her eyes, no longer Rebecca Randall's, mirrored Charlotte Corday's terrible agony.

"Ain't it lovely?" sighed Emma Jane as she admired the homemade prison.

"I hate to have to take it down," said Alice. "It's been such hard work."

"If you could move up some stones and just take off the top rows, I could step over," suggested Rebecca. "Then we can leave the stones, and you two can step down into the prison tomorrow and be the two little princes in the Tower, and I can murder you."

"What princes? What tower?" asked Alice and Emma Jane in one breath. "Tell us about them."

"Not now, it's my supper time." Rebecca had no intention of upsetting Aunt Miranda by being late for meals.

"It would be elegant being murdered by you," said Emma Jane loyally, "though you are awful real when you murder. Perhaps we could have Elijah and Elisha for the princes."

"They'd yell when they were murdered," objected Alice. "You know how silly the Simpsons are at plays, all except Clara Belle. Besides, if we once show them this secret place, they'll play in it all the time, and perhaps they'd steal things, like their father does."

"They needn't steal just because their father does," argued Rebecca, "and don't either of you ever talk about it in front of them if you want to be my secret, particular friends. My mother told me never to say hard things about people's folks to their faces. She says nobody can bear it, and it's wicked to shame people for what isn't their fault."

It was true, of course, that Abner Simpson had an awkward habit of "swapping" farm implements and vehicles of various kinds that usually belonged to his neighbors. After each of these "trades" he usually spent some time in jail.

That's where he was at the moment. He had taken the Widow Rideout's sleigh and exchanged it for Joseph Goodwin's plough. Goodwin had lately moved away so nobody knew if he had missed his plough, but after a time the Widow Rideout had missed her sleigh.

All the Riverboro children had heard about the missing sleigh and Abner Simpson's connection with it.

In school they soon began to make up riddles and bits of verse about the Simpson affair. They passed these around among themselves quite freely, but they were careful not to say them when the Simpson children were in the group.

Though Rebecca had been brought up much the same as her schoolmates, she hated gossip and refused to take part in it.

Alice and Emma Jane knew that Rebecca had had a terrible fight with a girl who had teased the Simpson children about their father. The girl was Minnie Smellie, who was generally disliked and distrusted by her classmates. She was suspected of copying answers from other girls' slates, although she had never been caught in the act. Rebecca and Emma Jane always knew when she had something especially good to eat in her lunch pail, because on those days she slipped away from her classmates and ate alone in the woods.

After one of these private luncheons, Rebecca could not control herself any longer.

When Minnie took her seat in the class, Rebecca asked, "Is your headache better, Minnie? Let me wipe that strawberry jam off your face."

There was no jam, but Minnie's handkerchief flew to her face in a flash.

Later that afternoon Rebecca confessed to Emma Jane that she was ashamed of her prank. "I do hate Minnie's ways, but I'm sorry I let her know we suspected her. To make up, I gave her that little piece of coral I keep in my bead purse."

"It hardly seems as if she deserved that, and her so greedy," remarked Emma Jane.

"I know it, but it made me feel better," said Rebecca, and the gift of coral did seem to smooth matters between the girls.

Several days later Rebecca, who had stayed after school as usual for her grammar lesson, took the shortcut home. Far ahead, she saw the Simpson children entering the woods. Seesaw was not with them, so she hurried to catch up and walk home with them. The children were hidden from sight by the trees when she heard Minnie Smellie's voice lifted high in song, and the sound of a child's sobbing. When she caught up with them, Clara Belle, Susan, and the twins were running

along the path, and Minnie Smellie was dancing up and down, shrieking:

"'What made the sleigh love Simpson so?'
    The eager children cried;
'Why Simpson loved the sleigh, you know,'
    The teacher quick replied."

As the Simpson children fled, Elijah threw
a stone at Minnie but it did not come within a
hundred yards of her. She was shouting "Jail
Birds" at the top of her lungs. Then she
wheeled about to meet Rebecca, who was
standing perfectly still in the path, her eyes
blazing.

"Minnie Smellie! If ever — I — catch — you
— singing — that — to the Simpsons again —
do you know what I'll do?" Rebecca was in a
rage.

"I don't know and I don't care," Minnie
said boldly, though she didn't look so bold.

"I'll take that piece of coral away from
you, and I think I shall slap you besides!"

"You wouldn't dare," retorted Minnie. "If
you do, I'll tell my mother and the teacher, so
there!"

"I don't care if you tell your mother, my
mother, and all your relations," said Rebecca,

gaining courage. "I don't care if you tell the town, the whole of York County, the state of Maine and — and the nation!" she finished grandly. "Now you remember what I say. If you do it again, and especially if you say 'jail birds,' I'll make you sorry somehow."

The next morning at recess, Rebecca heard Minnie telling the tale with variations to Huldah Meserve. "She *threatened* me," whispered Minnie, "but I never believe a word she says."

Minnie whispered loudly so that she would be overheard, for she had moments of bravery when she knew the teacher was near.

As Rebecca went back to her seat she dropped a note on Minnie's desk. This was the note she wrote:

Of all the girls that are so mean
There's none like Minnie Smellie.
I'll take away the gift I gave
And pound her into jelly.

P.S. *Now do you believe me?* R. Randall

For days afterward the rhyme had its effect on Minnie. Whenever she met the Simpsons, even a mile from the brick house, she held her peace.

Color of Rose

*F*RIDAY AFTERNOONS at school were always reserved for recitations — dialogues, songs, and poems. Most of the children hated learning these "speaking" pieces, and dreaded the danger of getting up to recite and forgetting the words. But for Rebecca it was the high point of the week.

On the Friday following her fight with Minnie, Rebecca was prepared to add some excitement and fun to the usual program. She had taught Elijah and Elisha Simpson three verses of a song. She gave Susan Simpson, who lisped, a funny poem in which she spoke like a lisping child, and she boosted Emma Jane's confidence by learning a dialogue with her that they would recite together.

On Friday morning Miss Dearborn announced that the program promised to be so interesting she had invited a number of important people in the community to attend. Then she asked Living Perkins to decorate one of the blackboards and Rebecca the other.

Living, who was the star artist of the school, chose to draw a map of North America. Rebecca drew an American flag in red, white, and blue chalk, with every star in place, every stripe fluttering in the breeze, and the figure of Columbia beside it.

Alice Robinson proposed that during the afternoon program the school should sing "Three Cheers for the Red, White, and Blue!" and when they came to the chorus, point to Rebecca's flag. Dick Carter suggested that the artists sign their names to their pictures, so that the visitors would know who drew them.

Miss Dearborn dismissed the morning session early so that those who lived nearby could go home to change their clothes. Emma Jane and Rebecca ran nearly every step of the way.

"Will your Aunt Miranda let you wear your best dress?" asked Emma Jane.

"I think I'll ask Aunt Jane," Rebecca replied. "Oh, if my pink was only finished! I left Aunt Jane making the buttonholes!"

"I'm going to ask my mother to let me wear her garnet ring," said Emma Jane. "It would look perfectly elegant flashing in the sun when I point to the flag. Good-bye! Don't wait for me going back. I may get a ride."

Rebecca found the side door of the brick house locked, but she knew that the key was under the step. She unlocked the door and went into the dining room to find her lunch laid on the table and a note from Aunt Jane saying that they had gone out driving with Mrs. Robinson. Rebecca swallowed a piece of bread and butter, and flew up the front stairs to her bedroom. On the bed lay the pink gingham dress, finished by Aunt Jane's kind hands. Dare she wear it without asking?

"I'll wear it," decided Rebecca. "They're not here to ask, and maybe they wouldn't mind a bit. It's only gingham after all."

She combed her hair, tied it back with a ribbon, changed her shoes, and slipped on the dress.

Then her eyes fell on her beloved pink sunshade. It matched her dress exactly. It wasn't quite appropriate for school, but she could just show it to the girls and carry it coming home. She glanced at herself in the parlor mirror and was overjoyed at how beautiful the dress looked. Goodness! It was twenty minutes to one. She danced out the side door, pulled a pink rose from a bush at the gate, and quickly covered the mile between the brick house and the school. Emma Jane met her at the entrance.

"Rebecca Randall!" she exclaimed. "You're pretty as a picture!"

Rebecca laughed. "It's only the pink gingham."

"How on earth did you get your Aunt Mirandy to let you put on your brand-new dress?"

"They were both away and I didn't ask," Rebecca responded anxiously. "Why? Do you think they'd have said no?"

"Miss Mirandy always says no, doesn't she?" asked Emma Jane.

"Ye-es, but this afternoon is very special — almost like a Sunday-school concert."

Emma Jane agreed. "Of course it is. With your name on the board, and our pointing to your flag, and our elegant dialogue, and all that...."

The afternoon was a triumph for everybody. Miss Dearborn heard many admiring remarks about her ability, and wondered whether they weren't due in part, at least, to Rebecca.

Though she had no more to do than anyone else, Rebecca was somehow in the foreground. No one could have called her "pushy," for she was eager to bring others into whatever fun there was, but she was ready, willing, and remarkably lacking in self-consciousness. As she strolled home, there were clouds gathering in the sky, but she hardly noticed them. She did not walk on solid ground at all until she entered the side yard of the brick house and saw Aunt Miranda standing in the open doorway. Then with a rush she came back to earth.

"There she is, over an hour late. A little more and she'd have been caught in a thunder shower," Miranda said to Jane. "And if she ain't rigged out in that new dress, swinging her parasol for all the world as if she was playacting. Now I'm the oldest, Jane, an' I intend to have my say. If you don't like it, you can go into the kitchen till it's over. Step right in here, Rebecca! I want to talk to you. Why did you put on that good new dress on a school day without permission?"

"I had intended to ask you at noontime, but you weren't home, so I couldn't," began Rebecca.

"You did no such a thing. You put it on because you were left alone, though you knew well enough I wouldn't have let you."

"If I'd been certain you wouldn't have let me, I'd never have done it," said Rebecca, trying to be truthful. "But I wasn't certain, and it was worth risking. I thought perhaps you might if you knew we were almost having a real exhibition at school."

"Exhibition!" exclaimed Miranda scornfully. "You are exhibition enough by yourself, I should say. Were you exhibiting your parasol?"

"The parasol was silly," confessed Rebecca, "but it's the only time in my whole life that I had anything to match it. It looked so beautiful with the pink dress! I haven't hurt my dress a mite, Aunt Mirandy."

"It's your underhandedness that's the worst," Miranda said coldly. "And look at the other things you've done! You went up the front stairs to your room. I knew, for you dropped your handkerchief on the way. You never cleared away your lunch and left the side door unlocked from half past twelve to three o'clock. Anybody could have come in and stolen what they liked!"

Rebecca sat down heavily in a chair. How could she have been so careless? The tears began to flow down her cheeks as she tried to explain.

"Oh, I'm so sorry!" she faltered. "I was helping decorate the schoolroom, and it got late and I ran all the way home. It was hard getting into my dress alone, and I hadn't time to eat but a mouthful. Then just at the last minute, when I honestly — honestly — thought about clearing away and locking up, I looked at the clock and knew I could hardly get back to school in time to form in the line."

"Don't wail and carry on now. It's no good crying over spilt milk," answered Miranda. "Instead of trying to see how little trouble you can make in a house that ain't your own home, it seems as if you try to see how much you can put us out. Take that rose out of your dress. I ain't got any patience with your flowers and frizzled out hair — and airs and graces for all the world like your fancy father."

Rebecca lifted her head in a flash. "Look here, Aunt Mirandy, I'll be as good as I know how to be. I'll mind when I'm spoken to and never leave the door unlocked again, but I won't have my father called names. He was a perfectly lovely father, that's what he was, and it's mean to call him fancy!"

"Don't you dare answer me back in that impudent way, Rebecca. Your father was a vain, foolish, shiftless man, and you might as well hear it from me as anybody else. He spent your mother's money and left her with seven children to provide for."

"It's s-something to leave s-seven nice children," sobbed Rebecca.

"Not when other folks have to help feed, clothe, and educate them," responded Miranda. "Go to your room, and stay there till tomorrow morning. You'll find a bowl of crackers and milk on your bureau, and I don't want to hear a sound from you till breakfast time. Jane, run and take the dish towels off the line. We're going to have a terrible shower."

"We've had it, I should think," Jane said quietly after Rebecca had left. "I don't often speak my mind, Mirandy, but you ought not to have said what you did about Lorenzo Randall. He was what he was, and can't be made any different, but he was Rebecca's father."

"The truth needs an airing now and then," Miranda said grimly. "That child will never amount to a hill of beans till she gets some of her father trounced out of her. I'm glad I said just what I did."

"I daresay you are," remarked Jane in a rare burst of courage. "But all the same, Mirandy, it wasn't good manners and it wasn't good religion!"

At that moment a clap of thunder shook the house. But it did not make as loud a noise in Miranda Sawyer's ears as Jane's remark. Her sister's words fell with a deafening roar on her conscience.

Rebecca climbed the back stairs, closed the door of her bedroom, and took off her beloved pink dress with trembling fingers. She smoothed it out carefully, pinched up the white ruffle at the neck, and laid it away in a drawer with a sob.

While she braided her hair an idea began to grow in her mind — to leave the brick house and go back to the farm. She would not be received there with open arms but she promised herself she would help her mother about the house and send Hannah to Riverboro in her place. "I hope she'll like it!" Rebecca thought in a burst of spite.

She sat by the window, trying to make some sort of plan, watching the streams of rain chasing one another down the lightning rod.

This was the day that had dawned so joyfully. How she had hoped that Aunt Miranda might be pleased that she had succeeded so well at school. But no, there was no hope of pleasing her aunt in that or in any other way. She would go to Maplewood on the stage next day with Mr. Cobb and somehow get home from Cousin Ann's. On second thought, her aunts might not allow it. Very well, she would slip away now and see if she could stay all night with the Cobbs and be off next morning before breakfast.

Rebecca never thought long over a decision. She put on her oldest clothes, then wrapped her nightdress and toothbrush in a bundle and dropped them softly out of the window. Her room was in the L of the house and her window was not far from the ground, though if it *had* been, nothing could have stopped her at that moment. She knew there was a cleat nailed to the side of the house, halfway between her window and the top of the back porch.

Rebecca listened carefully for a moment. When she heard the sound of the sewing machine in the dining room and chopping in the kitchen, she scrambled out of the window, slid down to the cleat, jumped to the top of the porch, used the woodbine trellis for a ladder, and was flying up the road in the storm before she had time to plan her next move.

Rainbow Bridges

JEREMIAH COBB sat alone at his supper. His wife was away for the evening, taking care of a sick neighbor. Looking up from his cup of tea, he saw Rebecca standing at the open door. Her face was so swollen with tears and so sharp with misery that for a moment he scarcely recognized her.

"Please may I come in, Mr. Cobb?" she asked in a mournful voice.

"Well I vow!" he cried. "It's my little lady passenger! Come to call and pass the time of day, have ye? Why, you're soaking wet. Draw up to the stove. I made a fire. We'll hang your soppy hat on the nail, put your jacket over the chair, and then you turn your back to the stove and dry yourself good."

Jeremiah Cobb had never before said so many words at one time, but when he caught sight of Rebecca's eyes and tear-stained cheeks, his heart went out to her.

Rebecca waited until he sat down again at the table. Then, unable to contain herself any longer, she cried, "Mr. Cobb, I've run away from the brick house. I want to go back to the farm. Will you keep me tonight and take me up to Maplewood on the stage tomorrow? I haven't got any money for my fare, but I'll earn it somehow afterward."

"Well, we won't quarrel about money," said the old man. "We've never had our ride together anyway, though we always meant to go down river, not up."

"I shall never see Milltown now!" sobbed Rebecca.

"Come sit over here on the footstool beside me and tell me all about it," he coaxed.

Rebecca leaned her head against Mr. Cobb's knee and poured out her troubles.

Mr. Cobb coughed and stirred in his chair a good deal while Rebecca spoke, but he carefully concealed his feelings of sympathy.

"You will take me to Maplewood, won't you, Mr. Cobb?" begged Rebecca.

"Don't you fret a mite," he soothed her, while a crafty idea was forming at the back of his mind. "Now take a bite of something to eat, child. Draw up to the table. How'd you like to sit in Mother's place and pour me out another cup of hot tea?"

Rebecca felt comforted by the old man's tone. She lifted the blue china teapot, smiled faintly, smoothed her hair, and dried her eyes.

"I suppose your mother'll be terrible glad to see you back again?" said Mr. Cobb, knowing full well what the answer would be.

A tiny fear stirred in the bottom of Rebecca's heart the moment he asked the question.

"She won't like it that I ran away, I suppose, and she'll be sorry that I couldn't please Aunt Mirandy. But I'll make her understand."

"I suppose she was thinking of your schooling, when she sent you down here. But land! You can go to school in Temperance, can't you?"

"There's only two months of school now in Temperance, and the farm's too far from other schools."

"Oh, well, there's other things in the world besides education," responded Mr. Cobb, attacking a piece of apple pie.

"Ye-es, though Mother thought it was going to be the making of me," Rebecca replied sadly, as she tried to drink her tea.

"It'll be nice for you to be all together

again at the farm — such a house full of children," remarked the clever old man.

"It's too full — that's the trouble. But I'll make Hannah come to Riverboro in my place."

"Do you suppose Mirandy and Jane'll have her? I should be almost afraid they wouldn't. They'll be kind of mad at your going home, you know, and you can't hardly blame 'em."

This was quite a new thought — that the brick house might be closed to Hannah if Rebecca turned her back on it.

"How is the school down here in Riverboro — pretty good?" inquired Mr. Cobb, whose brain was working at an unusually rapid pace.

"Oh, it's a splendid school. And Miss Dearborn is a splendid teacher."

"You like her, do you? Well, believe me she returns the compliment. Just this afternoon Mother met her on the bridge and they got to talking about school. 'I could teach school from sunup to sundown if my pupils was all like Rebecca Randall,' says she."

"Oh, Mr. Cobb, *did* she say that?" Rebecca's face glowed. "I've tried hard all the time, but I'll study the covers right off the books now."

"You mean you could if you was going to

stay here," corrected Mr. Cobb. "Too bad you've got to give it all up on account of your Aunt Mirandy. Well, I can't hardly blame ye. She's cranky and she's sour. She needs bearing with and I guess you ain't much on patience, are ye?"

"Not very much," Rebecca admitted.

"If I'd had this talk with ye yesterday," Mr. Cobb went on, "I believe I'd have advised you different. It's too late now though. I don't mean to say you've been all in the wrong, but if 'twas to do over again, well ... your Aunt Mirandy gives you clothes and board and schooling and is going to send you to Wareham at a big expense. She's terrible hard to get along with and kind of heaves benefits at your head, same as she would bricks, but they're benefits just the same. Jane's a little bit more easy going than Mirandy, ain't she? Or is she just as hard to please?"

"Oh, Aunt Jane and I get along splendidly," exclaimed Rebecca. "She's good and kind and I like her better all the time. I think she kind of likes me too. I'd let her scold me all day long, for she understands. But she can't stand up for me against Aunt Mirandy. She's about as afraid of her as I am."

"Jane'll be real sorry tomorrow to find you've gone away. But never mind, it can't be helped. Mother was talking with her after prayer meeting the other night. 'You wouldn't know the brick house, Sarah,' says Jane. 'I'm keeping a sewing school, and my student has made three dresses. And I've taken a class in Sunday school, and I'm thinking of going to the picnic with Rebecca.' Mother declares she never did see Jane look so happy."

There was a silence in the little kitchen that was broken only by the ticking of the tall clock. Outside the rain had stopped.

"The shower's over," said the old man, filling his pipe. "It's cleared the air. Tomorrow everything will shine like a new pin when you and I are driving up the river."

Rebecca rose from the table, and put on her hat and jacket. "I'm not going to drive up-river, Mr. Cobb," she said. "I'm going to stay here and catch bricks! Catch 'em without throwing 'em back too. I don't know as Aunt Mirandy will take me back after I've run away, but I'm going to ask her now, while I have the courage. You wouldn't be so good as to go with me would you, Mr. Cobb?"

"You'd better believe your Uncle Jerry don't intend to leave you till he gets this thing fixed up," cried the old man delightedly. "Mirandy'll be sore and cross and in no condition for argument so my plan is just this: I'll drive you over to the brick house in my buggy, and have you sit back in the corner. I'll get out and go to the side door. When I get your Aunt Mirandy and Aunt Jane out in the shed, to plan for a load of wood I'm going to have hauled there this week, you'll slip out of the buggy and go upstairs to bed. The front door won't be locked, will it?"

"Not this time of night," Rebecca answered. "Not till Aunt Mirandy goes to bed. But what if it should be?"

"Well, it won't. And if it is, why we'll have to face it out. In my opinion you ain't run away yet. You've only come over here to consult me about running away, an' we've concluded it ain't worth the trouble. The only bad thing you've done, as I figure it, was to come here by the window when you'd been sent to bed. And that ain't so very bad. But I don't believe in deceiving folks, so you can tell your Aunt Jane about it later. She can advise you about how to tell your Aunt Mirandy. Now come on, I'm all hitched up to go over to the post office. Don't forget your bundle."

When Rebecca crept upstairs and finally got into bed that night, she was aching in every nerve, but she felt a kind of peace steal over her. She knew that Mr. Cobb had saved her from doing a foolish thing. She was determined to win Aunt Miranda's approval and try to forget the one thing that hurt the most — the scornful mention of her father, whom she thought of with the greatest admiration.

It would have been some comfort to Rebecca to know that Miranda Sawyer was passing an uncomfortable night. She regretted her harshness, partly because Jane had taken a firm position in the matter, and she could not endure Jane's disapproval, although she would never have confessed to such a weakness.

"I never saw a child improve so in her work as Rebecca has today," Miranda remarked to Jane the next evening. "That scolding I gave her was probably just what she needed."

"I'm glad you're pleased," Jane replied. "A cringing worm is what you want, not a bright, smiling child. Rebecca looks to me as if she's been through the Seven Years' War. If you follow my advice, which you seldom do, you'll let her go to the fair in Milltown with the Cobbs and Perkinses. Maybe that'll cheer her up a little and coax back her appetite."

Double Trouble

*R*EBECCA WENT TO THE FAIR in Milltown and it was all that her vivid imagination had painted. Both she and Emma Jane had never spent a day so crowded with wonderful things to see, to eat, and to do.

"She's the best company I ever saw in all my life," Mrs. Cobb said to her husband that evening. "Did you watch her face when we went into that tent where they was acting out *Uncle Tom's Cabin*? And did you notice the way she told us about the book when we sat down to have ice cream? I tell you the author, Harriet Beecher Stowe herself, couldn't have done it better."

"I took it all in," answered Mr. Cobb, who was pleased that his wife agreed with him about Rebecca. "I ain't sure but she's going to turn out to be something remarkable — maybe a singer, or a writer."

But there was an incident after Rebecca saw the play in Milltown that caused her some trouble during the next week. Minnie Smellie's mother told Miranda Sawyer that Rebecca had been overheard swearing and using profane language to Emma Jane and Living Perkins, and that those two laughed, and chased her.

When Rebecca was charged with this, she denied it indignantly, and Aunt Jane believed her.

"Search your memory, Rebecca, and try to remember what Minnie could have heard you say," Aunt Jane pleaded. "Don't be obstinate, but think real hard."

A sudden light broke over Rebecca's face.

"Oh! I know now," she exclaimed. "We were coming home from school. It had rained and the road was full of puddles. Emma Jane, Living, and I were walking along, and I was ahead. I saw the water streaming over the road toward the ditch, and it reminded me of *Uncle Tom's Cabin*, when Eliza took her baby and ran across the Mississippi on the ice blocks, chased by the bloodhounds.

"I knew Living and Emma Jane would remember, too, so I took off my waterproof and wrapped it around my books for a baby. Then I shouted, '*My God! The river!*' just like Eliza did in the play. Then I leaped from puddle to puddle, and Living and Emma Jane pursued me like the bloodhounds. It's just like that stupid Minnie Smellie not to know a game when she sees one. And Eliza wasn't swearing when she said 'My God! The river!' It was more like praying."

"Well, you've got no call to be praying or swearing, in the middle of the road," said Miranda. "But I'm thankful it's no worse. You're born to trouble and I'm afraid you always will be till you learn to bridle your unruly tongue."

"I wish sometimes that I could bridle Minnie's," murmured Rebecca, as she went to set the table for supper.

"I declare. She *is* the oddest child," said Miranda, laying down her mending. "You don't think she's a little mite crazy, do you, Jane?"

"I don't think she's like the rest of us," Jane replied thoughtfully, with some anxiety in her pleasant face, "but whether it's for the better or the worse I can't tell till she grows up. Rebecca's got the makings of almost any-

72

thing in her, but I feel sometimes as if we were not fitted to cope with her."

"Stuff and nonsense!" said Miranda. "Speak for yourself. I feel fitted to cope with any child that ever was born into the world!"

"I know you do, Mirandy, but that don't *make* you so," returned Jane with a smile.

The habit of speaking her mind freely was growing on Jane to a terrifying extent.

It wasn't long before Rebecca was once again in trouble. She was wearing her best dress and was on her way to tea with the Cobbs. As she strolled across the bridge, she was suddenly overcome by the beauty of the river. Leaning her body against the railing she stood dreaming and putting the finishing touches on a poem.

Suddenly she jumped back. "Oh! Paint! It's all over my best dress! Oh! what *will* I do?"

With tears streaming from her eyes, Rebecca ran up the hill to the Cobbs' house for help.

Mrs. Cobb took in the situation at a glance, and vowed that she could remove almost any stain from almost any fabric.

The dress was removed and partially dipped in turpentine, while Rebecca sat at the table clad in a blue calico wrapper of Mrs. Cobb's.

"Don't let it take your appetite away," crooned Mrs. Cobb. "I've got cream biscuit and honey for you. If the turpentine don't work, I'll try French chalk, magnesia, and warm suds. If they fail, Father shall borrow some of the stuff Marthy Strout got in Milltown to take the currant pie out of her wedding dress."

"I don't understand this painting accident yet," said Mr. Cobb, as he handed Rebecca the honey. "There's fresh paint signs hung all over the bridge."

"I didn't notice the signs," Rebecca said sadly. "I suppose I was looking at the river."

When tea was cleared away Rebecca insisted on doing the dishes, while Mrs. Cobb worked on her dress. As it began to look a little better, Rebecca's spirits lifted. When the dress was hung out in the air to dry, everyone went into the sitting room.

"Have you a piece of paper, please?" asked Rebecca. "I'll write out the poem I was composing while I was leaning on the paint."

Mrs. Cobb sat down to mend and Mr. Cobb settled himself in his favorite chair.

Rebecca soon had the poem written, and she read it aloud:

THE TWO WISHES
by
Rebecca Randall

Two maidens by a river strayed,
   'Twas in the state of Maine.
Rebecca was the darker one,
   The fairer, Emma Jane.
The fairer maiden said, "I would
   My life were as the stream;
So peaceful and so smooth and still
   So pleasant and serene."

"I'd rather be a little drop
   In the great rushing fall;
I'd never choose the quiet lake;
   'Twould not please me at all."
(It was the darker maiden spoke
   The words we just have stated;
The maidens twain were simply friends,
   Not sisters, or related.)

But O! alas! we may not have
   The things we hope to gain.
The quiet life may come to me,
   The rush to Emma Jane!

The Cobbs thought Rebecca's poem was marvelous.

"How in the world do you do it?" Mrs. Cobb exclaimed.

"Oh, it's easy," answered Rebecca. "The hymns at meeting are all like that. There's a school newspaper printed at Wareham Academy* once a month called *The Pilot*, and Dick Carter at school says girls are allowed to try and write for it. The editor is always a boy, of course. Dick thinks I'm good enough to get in it."

"In it!" exclaimed Mr. Cobb. "I shouldn't be a bit surprised if you could write the whole paper."

"Can we have a copy of the poem to keep in the family Bible?" inquired Mrs. Cobb.

"Would you like it?" asked Rebecca. "Yes, indeed! I'll do a nice one with violet ink and a fine pen. But I must go and look at my poor dress."

Rebecca's dress was quite dry and had been improved a little, but the colors had run in the rubbing and the pattern was blurred. As a last resort, Mrs. Cobb ironed it carefully and Rebecca put the dress on so that they might see the final result.

The spots showed clearly. Rebecca took one good look at them and said, "I think I'll be

*In Maine, some high schools are still called academies.

going. Good night! If I've got to have a scolding, I want it quick, and get it over."

Rebecca took her scolding, and there was a lot of it. Miranda remarked, among other things that so absentminded a child was sure to grow up into a driveling idiot.

When Rebecca reached her room, she began to think. If there was anything she did not wish to become, it was an idiot of any sort, particularly a driveling one. She resolved to punish herself every time she did something that displeased her aunt.

She considered the value of wearing a piece of haircloth next to her skin, and a pebble in her shoe, but dismissed both ideas. The haircloth could not be found and the pebble would attract the notice of her sharp-eyed aunt, besides making it difficult to walk almost a mile to school.

She looked about her room as she sat by the window searching for some other form of self-punishment. She must give up something, and the truth was she possessed little to give up, except her beloved pink parasol. But she could not hide it in the attic, for in a moment of weakness she was sure to take it out again and she did not have the courage to break it into bits. Her eyes moved from the parasol to the window, and then fell on the well. That was it. She would fling her dearest possession into the depths of the water.

As always, action followed quickly upon decision. Rebecca slipped downstairs in the darkness, stole out the front door, walked to the well, lifted the cover, and with a shudder, flung the parasol downward with all her force.

That night she slept well, arose refreshed, and went on her way to school. But at home, her aunts had great difficulty in drawing water from the well after breakfast, and Abijah Flagg had to be summoned. He lifted the well cover, explored, found the parasol jammed into the side of the well, and removed it.

When poor Rebecca had to explain the reasons behind the sacrifice of her sunshade, Aunt Miranda said, "Now see here, Rebecca. When you think you ain't been punished enough, just tell me and I'll invent a little something more. I ain't as smart as some folks, but I can do that much, and whatever it is, it'll be something that won't make the whole family drink ivory dust, wood chips, and pink silk rags with their water."

Mr. Aladdin

JUST BEFORE THANKSGIVING the affairs of
the Simpson family reached a crisis. There
was little to eat in the household and less to
wear, though Mrs. Simpson did her best by
taking in wash and cleaning house for women
in the village. The children managed to get a
little more to eat by sitting outside their
neighbors' kitchen doors when meals were
about to be served.

As the gloomy days of November set in,
and they were approaching a cheerless
Thanksgiving, the Simpsons began to look
about for some inexpensive way to brighten
the holidays. They decided to try once again
to sell soap for the Excelsior Soap Company,
which paid them very little, but gave premiums for the sale of so many cakes of soap.
The year before they had sold enough soap to
their neighbors to get a wagon. Now they

wanted to expand their operations to get a better premium, but they needed a larger sales staff.

At this point Clara Belle and Susan Simpson consulted Rebecca, who threw herself wholeheartedly into the project, promising that both she and Emma Jane Perkins would help.

After a careful study of the premiums in the company's colorful circular, it was decided that the Simpsons would get the most benefit from a banquet lamp. The elaborate brass table lamp soon became more desirable to them than food, drink, or clothing. Neither Emma Jane nor Rebecca could see anything strange in the idea of a poor family like the Simpsons striving for such a lamp. Every day they looked at the pictures in the circular and knew that if they had been allowed to, they would toil, suffer, and sweat to own such a lamp.

There was more fun than hard work as the girls prepared to become salesmen. A long meeting was held in Emma Jane's attic to practice their selling techniques. They used the soap company's circular, which had a sample of an "effective" sales speech, and they copied the method and style of a patent-medicine salesman they had heard at the

Milltown Fair. Emma Jane practiced the speech on Rebecca, and Rebecca on Emma Jane.

"Can I sell you a little soap this afternoon?" Emma Jane began. "It is called the Snow-White and Rose-Red Soap, six cakes in an ornamental box, only twenty cents for the white, twenty-five for the red. It is made from the purest ingredients, and if desired could be eaten by an invalid with relish and profit." At this point Emma Jane stopped and pleaded with Rebecca. "Oh, don't let's say that! It makes me feel like a fool."

"It takes so little to make you feel like a fool, Emma Jane," rebuked Rebecca. "I don't get to feeling like a fool as easily. Leave out the eating part, if you don't like it, and go on."

"Snow-White is probably the most remarkable laundry soap ever manufactured," Emma Jane continued. "Immerse your garments in a tub. Lightly rub the more soiled portions with the soap, leave them submerged in water from sunset to sunrise, and the youngest baby can wash them without the slightest effort."

"*Babe*, not baby," corrected Rebecca, reading from the circular.

"It's the same thing," argued Emma Jane.

"Of course it's the same *thing;* but babe or infant sounds better. Would you rather say infant?"

"No," grumbled Emma Jane. "Infant is even worse than babe. Rebecca, do you think we'd better do as the circular says, and let Elijah or Elisha try the soap before we begin selling?"

"I can't imagine a babe doing a family wash with *any* soap," answered Rebecca, "but it must be true or they would never dare to print it, so don't let's bother. Oh, won't it be fun, Emma Jane? At the houses where they can't possibly know me, I shan't be frightened and I shall reel off the whole rigmarole, invalid, babe, and all. Perhaps I shall even say the last sentence, if I can remember it: 'We sound every chord in the great macro-cosm of satisfaction.' "

That weekend Rebecca stayed at Emma Jane's house while her aunts went to Portland to attend the funeral of an old friend. On Saturday the girls asked Mrs. Perkins if they could take the horse and wagon and call at a few houses in North Riverboro to sell some soap. At first she refused to give her permission. She had little objection if Emma Jane amused herself in this unusual way. It was for Rebecca, the niece of the difficult Miranda

Sawyer, that she was concerned. When she was fully persuaded that the work was a charitable venture, she gave her consent.

The girls drove to Mr. Watson's grocery store, where they picked up several large boxes of soap, and had no trouble charging them to Clara Belle Simpson's account. Mr. Watson had been told about the Simpson children's plans. The boxes were lifted into the back of the wagon, and the girls drove off along the country road ready for adventure.

After one hour of trying to sell soap, their spirits began to droop.

"It's your turn, Rebecca, and I'm glad," said Emma Jane, drawing up to a gateway and indicating a house that was set back from the road. "I don't know who lives here, and the blinds are all shut in front. If there's nobody at home you have to take the next house too."

Rebecca walked up the path to the side door. There was a porch there, and seated in a rocking chair, husking corn, was a good-looking young man — or was he middle-aged? Rebecca could not make up her mind. She did decide that he had the air of the city about him — a well-shaven face, well-trimmed mustache, and well-fitting clothes. Rebecca was a trifle shy at this unexpected meeting, but there was nothing to do but explain her **presence**. "Is the lady of the house at home?" she asked.

"I am the lady of the house at present," said the stranger, with an amused smile. "What can I do for you?"

"Have you ever heard of the — would you like — I mean — do you need any soap?" Rebecca stumbled.

"Do I look as if I do?" he responded unexpectedly.

Rebecca laughed. "I didn't mean *that*. I have some soap to sell. I mean I would like to introduce to you a very remarkable soap, the best now on the market. It is called the — "

"Oh! I must know that soap," said the gentleman. "Made out of pure vegetable fat, isn't it?"

"The very purest," Rebecca agreed.

"No acid in it?"

"Not a trace."

"And yet a child could do the Monday washing with it and use no force."

"A babe," corrected Rebecca.

"Oh! a babe, eh? That child grows younger every year instead of older — wise child!"

This was great good fortune, to find a customer who knew all about her product in advance. Rebecca relaxed more and more, and at her new friend's invitation sat down on a stool near the edge of the porch. Presently she forgot all about her partner at the gate and was talking as if she had known this grand person all her life.

"I'm keeping house today, but I don't live here," explained the delightful gentleman. "I'm visiting my aunt, who has gone to Portland. I used to come here as a boy, and I am very fond of this place."

"I don't think anything takes the place of the farm where one lived when one was a child," observed Rebecca, nearly bursting with pride at having successfully used the indefinite pronoun in general conversation.

The man darted a look at her and put down an ear of corn. "So you consider your childhood a thing of the past, do you, young lady?"

"I can still remember it," answered Rebecca, "though it seems a long time ago."

"I can remember mine well enough, and a particularly unpleasant one it was," said the stranger.

"So was mine," sighed Rebecca. "What was your worst trouble?"

"Lack of food and clothes principally."

"Oh!" exclaimed Rebecca sympathetically. "Mine was no shoes and too many babies and not enough books. But you're all right and happy now, aren't you?" she asked. The man looked handsome, well-fed, and prosperous, she thought, but his eyes seemed sad when he was not speaking.

"I'm doing pretty well, thank you," said the man, with a smile. "Now tell me, how much soap should I buy today?"

"How much has your aunt on hand now" asked the inexperienced agent, "and how much would she need?"

"Oh, I don't know. Soap keeps, doesn't it?"

"I'm not certain," said Rebecca truthfully. "I'll look in the circular — it's sure to tell." She drew the document from her pocket.

"What are you going to do with the profits you get from this business?"

"We are not selling for our own benefit," Rebecca said confidentially. "My friend who is holding the horse at the gate, is the daughter of a very rich blacksmith, and doesn't need any money. I am poor, but I live with my aunts in a brick house, and of course they wouldn't like me to be a peddler. We are trying to get a premium for some friends of ours."

Rebecca had never thought of telling these facts to her previous customers, but suddenly she found herself describing the Simpson family — their poverty, and their great need for a banquet lamp to brighten their lives.

"You needn't explain that point," laughed the man, as he stood up to get a glimpse of the "rich blacksmith's daughter" at the gate. "I agree that they ought to have it if they want it, and especially if you want them to have it. I've known what it was to do without a banquet lamp. Now give me the circular, and let's do some figuring. How much do the Simpsons lack at this moment?"

"If they sell two hundred more cakes this month, they can have the lamp by Christmas," Rebecca answered, "and they can get a shade by summer time. I'm afraid I can't help very much after today, because my Aunt Miranda may not like me to."

"I see. Well, that's all right. I'll take three hundred cakes, and that will give them the shade and all."

Rebecca had been seated on a stool very near the edge of the porch. At this remark she made a sudden movement, tipped over, and disappeared into a clump of lilac bushes. It was a very short distance, fortunately, and her amused customer picked her up, set her on her feet, and brushed her off. "You should never act surprised when you have taken a large order," he said. "You should have replied, 'Can't you make it three hundred and fifty?' instead of capsizing in that unbusinesslike way."

"Oh, I could never say anything like that!" exclaimed Rebecca, who was blushing at her awkward fall. "But it doesn't seem right for you to buy so much. Are you sure you can afford it?"

"If I can't, I'll save on something else," returned her joking benefactor.

"What if your aunt shouldn't like this kind of soap?" Rebecca asked nervously.

"My aunt always likes what I like," he returned.

"Mine doesn't!" exclaimed Rebecca.

"Then there's something wrong with your aunt!"

"Or with me," laughed Rebecca.

"What is your name, young lady?"

"Rebecca Rowena Randall, sir."

"What," he smiled with amusement. "Two names? Your mother was generous."

"She couldn't bear to give up either of the names, she says."

"Do you want to hear my name?"

"I think I know already," Rebecca answered, with a bright glance. "I'm sure you must be Mr. Aladdin in the *Arabian Nights*. Oh, please, can I run down and tell Emma Jane? She must be so tired of waiting and she will be so glad!"

At the man's nod, Rebecca sped down the lane, crying excitedly as she neared the wagon, "Oh, Emma Jane! Emma Jane! We are sold out!"

Mr. Aladdin followed her to confirm this astonishing, unbelievable statement. Then he lifted all the boxes from the back of the wagon and, taking the circular, promised to write to the Excelsior Company that night about the premium.

"If you two girls can keep a secret, I think I can manage to have the lamp arrive at the Simpson's on Thanksgiving Day. Wouldn't it be a nice surprise?" he asked, as he tucked the old lap robe over their feet.

They agreed wholeheartedly and broke into a chorus of excited thanks.

"Don't mention it!" laughed Mr. Aladdin, lifting his hat. "I was sort of a commercial traveler myself once, and I want to see the thing well done. Good-bye, Miss Rebecca Rowena! Just let me know whenever you have anything to sell, for I'm certain beforehand I shall want it."

"Good-bye, Mr. Aladdin! I surely will!" cried Rebecca, tossing back her dark braid delightedly and waving her hand.

"Oh, Rebecca!" said Emma Jane in an awestruck whisper. "He raised his hat to us, and we're not yet thirteen! It will be five years before we're ladies."

"Never mind," answered Rebecca, "we are the *beginning* of ladies, even now."

The Banquet Lamp

ON THANKSGIVING DAY there was company at the brick house. The Burnham sisters, who lived in North Riverboro, had come to dinner, as they had been doing for more than twenty-five years. After the dinner dishes were washed, Rebecca sat silent with a book until it was almost five, then asked if she might go to the Simpsons.

"Why do you want to go to the Simpsons?" asked Miranda. "Can't you sit still for once and listen to the conversation of your elders?"

"The Simpsons have a new lamp, and Emma Jane and I promised to go over and see it lighted, and make it a kind of a party."

"What do they want with a new lamp, and where did they get the money to pay for it? They haven't enough now to pay for candles."

"The children got it as a prize for selling

soap," replied Rebecca. "You know I told you that Emma Jane and I helped them the Saturday afternoon you were in Portland."

"I didn't take notice, I suppose. You can go for an hour, and no more," Miranda said. "Of all the foolishness," Miranda continued after Rebecca had left. "That lamp beats all. It's just like those Simpsons, but I didn't think the children had brains enough to sell anything."

"One of them must have," said Ellen Burnham. "Adam Ladd in North Riverboro said the girl who sold soap to him was the most remarkable and winning child he ever saw."

"It must have been Clara Belle, but I should never call her remarkable," answered Miranda. "Has Adam been home again?"

"Yes, he's been staying a few days with his aunt. She says he was so taken with the little girl who sold him the three hundred cakes of soap that he said he was going to bring her a Christmas present."

"Three hundred cakes of soap!" exclaimed Miranda. "Well, there's one crop that never fails in Riverboro!"

"What's that?" asked Lydia Burnham politely.

"The fool crop," Miranda snapped back, and changed the subject, much to her sister

Jane's relief. She had been nervous for the last few minutes, for she didn't think any child in Riverboro, except Rebecca, could be so remarkable and winning as to make anyone buy three hundred cakes of soap.

Outside, in the dusk, Rebecca flew up the road. She had not gone far before she saw Emma Jane coming toward her. In a moment they had met and given each other a breathless hug.

"Something awful has happened," panted Emma Jane.

"Don't tell me it's broken," exclaimed Rebecca.

"No, oh, no! Not that! It was packed in straw, and every piece came out all right. I was there and I never said a single thing about your selling the three hundred cakes that got the lamp, so that we could be together when you told."

"*Our* selling the three hundred cakes," corrected Rebecca. "You did as much as I did."

"No, I didn't, Rebecca Randall. I just sat at the gate and held the horse."

"Yes, but *whose* horse was it that took us to North Riverboro? But what's the trouble?"

"The Simpsons have no kerosene oil and no wicks. Seesaw has gone to the doctor's to borrow a wick, and Mother let me have a pint of oil. But she says she won't give me anymore. We never thought of the expense of keeping up the lamp, Rebecca."

"No, we didn't, but let's not worry about that till after the party."

By half past five the Simpsons' party was at its height. The banquet lamp had been placed on the one small table in the house, and its crimson paper shade glowed like a giant ruby. The family sat in the wide splash of light that it flung upon the floor, silently admiring its beauty. Rebecca and Emma Jane stood behind them, hand in hand, too thrilled to utter a word.

"I wish Father could see it," said Clara Belle.

"If he saw it he'd want to swap it," Susan murmured wisely.

At the end of the hour, Rebecca dragged herself away from the enchanting scene.

"I'll turn the lamp out the minute I think you and Emma Jane are home," said Clara Belle. "I'm so glad you both live where you can see it shine from our windows."

"We don't have to worry about kerosene," said Seesaw, coming in from the shed. "Mr. Tubbs just bought a big keg of it over from

94

North Riverboro. He said somebody ordered it by mail."

Rebecca squeezed Emma Jane's arm. "It was Mr. Aladdin," whispered Rebecca, as they ran down the path to the gate. Seesaw followed them and offered to see them down the road, but Rebecca thanked him and told him quite firmly that it wasn't necessary.

When Rebecca entered the brick house, the guests were gone and her aunts were knitting in the dining room.

"It was a heavenly party," she said, taking off her hat and cape. "Aunt Jane, Aunt Miranda, if you'll come into the kitchen and look out of the sink window, you can see the banquet lamp shining all red, just as if the Simpsons' house was on fire."

"And probably it will be before long," observed Miranda, without moving. "I've got no patience with such foolish going's-on."

Jane got up and followed Rebecca into the kitchen. Although the faint light she saw in the distance was not a dazzling exhibition, she tried to be as enthusiastic as possible. After which she turned to Rebecca and said, "Who sold the three hundred cakes of soap to Mr. Ladd in North Riverboro?"

"Mr. *Who*?" exclaimed Rebecca.

"Mr. Ladd, in North Riverboro."

"Is that his real name?" Rebecca asked in astonishment. "I didn't make a bad guess," she said, laughing to herself.

"I asked you who sold the soap to Adam Ladd?" repeated Jane.

"Adam Ladd! Then he's A. Ladd too. What fun!"

"Answer me, Rebecca."

"Excuse me, Aunt Jane, I was so busy thinking. Emma Jane and I sold the soap to Mr. Ladd."

"Did you make him buy it?"

"Now, Aunt Jane, how could I make a grown-up man buy anything if he didn't want to? He needed the soap for his aunt. He bought all we had and made us promise to keep the secret until the lamp came. I've been going about ever since as if it was inside of me all lighted up and burning for everybody to see."

"That's just the way you look — as if you did have a lamp burning inside of you." Aunt Jane sighed. "Rebecca! Rebecca! I wish you could take things easier, child. I am fearful for you, sometimes."

Season of Growth

*T*HE DAYS FLEW BY after Thanksgiving. Life in the brick house was going along more smoothly, for Rebecca was making a great effort not to upset her aunt and Miranda was trying not to lose her temper. But there was one outburst of wrath that Miranda could not control.

Late one Friday afternoon, Rebecca asked her aunt if she might take some bread and milk upstairs to a friend.

"What friend have you got up there, for pity's sake?" demanded Miranda.

"The Simpson baby — come to stay till Sunday. That is, if you're willing. Mrs. Simpson says she is. Shall I bring her down and show her to you?"

"You can bring her down, but you can't show her to me! You can smuggle her out the way you smuggled her in. Where on earth do you get your notions!"

"You're so used to a house without a baby you don't know how dull it is," sighed Rebecca, as she moved toward the door. "At the farm there were too many, but that's not half as bad as none at all. I'll take her back but she'll be dreadfully disappointed, and so will Mrs. Simpson. She was planning to go to Milltown."

"She can unplan then," snapped Miranda.

"Perhaps I can go up there and take care of the baby?" suggested Rebecca. "I brought her home so that I could do my Saturday work just the same."

"You've got enough to do right here, without any borrowed babies to make more work. Now, no answering back, just give the child some supper and take it home where it belongs."

Upstairs, Rebecca found Aunt Jane sorting out sheets in the linen closet, and sought comfort from her.

"I brought the Simpson baby home, Aunt Jane, thinking it would help us over a dull Sunday, but Aunt Miranda won't let her stay.

Come in and look at her sitting up in my bed. Isn't she lovely? She's the fat, gurgly kind, not thin and fussy like some babies. I thought I was going to have her to dress and undress twice each day. Oh dear! I wish I had a book with everything written down in it that I *could* do. Then I wouldn't get disappointed so often."

"No book could be written that would fit you, Rebecca," answered Aunt Jane, "for nobody could imagine the things you'd want to do. Are you going to carry that heavy child home in your arms?"

"No, I'm going to pull her in the soap-wagon. Come, baby!" Rebecca picked up the crowing baby, sat down in a chair with her, and prepared to dress her for the trip home.

Aunt Jane watched in amazement. Whether the baby was flat on her stomach, or head down and heels in the air, she knew that she was in the hands of an expert, and she gurgled placidly.

"Bless my soul, Rebecca," Aunt Jane said. "It beats all how handy you are with babies!"

"I ought to be. I've brought up three and a half of 'em," Rebecca said cheerfully, pulling up the infant's stockings.

"I should think you'd be fonder of dolls than you are," said Jane.

"I do like them, but there's never any change in a doll. It's always the same everlasting old doll, and you have to make believe it's cross or sick, or it loves you, or can't bear you. Babies are more trouble, but nicer."

Aunt Jane stretched out her hand and the baby curled her fingers around the worn gold ring that she wore on her finger.

"You wear a ring on your engagement finger, don't you, Aunt Jane? Did you ever think about getting married?"

"Yes, dear, long ago."

"What happened, Aunt Jane?"

"He died — just before."

"Oh!" Rebecca's eyes grew misty.

"He was a soldier and he died of a gunshot wound in a hospital down South."

"Oh! Aunt Jane!" Rebecca whispered. "Away from you?"

"No, I was with him."

"Was he young?"

"Yes, young and brave and handsome, Rebecca. He was Mr. Carter's brother Tom."

"I'm so glad you were with him. Wasn't he glad, Aunt Jane?"

Jane looked back across the half-forgotten

years and the memory of Tom's death was as clear to her as though it had happened yesterday. She had never before told anyone what it had meant to her, for there was no one in Riverboro who would have understood. To hide her tears, she put her head down on her niece's shoulder and said, "It was hard, Rebecca!"

Rebecca put her cheek against her aunt's gray hair. "I'm sorry, Aunt Jane."

Rebecca's eyes, too, filled with tears, for she shared the loneliness. Just that week Rebecca had received a letter from Sunnybrook Farm. It had been the thought of her family — her brothers and sisters — that had made her think of bringing the Simpson baby to the brick house for the weekend. Her mother had written that Hannah was wearing her hair up and her dresses a bit below her ankles. That Mark had broken his collarbone but was healing well, and that a new railroad line was to be built near the Randall farm, raising its value.

Best of all was the news about John, Rebecca's favorite brother. He had gone to live at their Cousin Ann's when she lost her husband, a kindly old doctor. John was to get an education in return for taking care of her farm, and what was most exciting, he could use the medical library that had belonged to Ann's husband. For a long time John's heart had been set on becoming a country doctor and having Rebecca keep house for him. Now it looked as though his dream might come true.

Rebecca felt both sad and happy. She felt suddenly a greater depth of understanding that is the start of being an adult.

Gray Days and Gold

*F*OR WEEKS BEFORE CHRISTMAS, Rebecca was busy making presents for everyone at Sunnybrook Farm. It was difficult, for she had managed to save only fifty cents, but her precious package of gifts had been sent off by mail two days before Christmas.

Rebecca's own gifts included a warm gray squirrel muff and scarf from Aunt Miranda and a lovely dress of soft green cashmere made for her by Aunt Jane. A beautiful lace collar had come from her mother, scarlet mittens from Mr. and Mrs. Cobb, and a handkerchief from Emma Jane.

For her aunts, Rebecca had designed and sewn an elaborate tea cozy with the letter M in outline stitch, and a pretty frilled pincushion marked with a J.

On Christmas morning there was an unexpected knock at the door at breakfast time.

103

Rebecca answered it. A young boy asked if Miss Rebecca Randall lived there, and on being told that she did, handed her a parcel bearing her name. She took the package and returned to the dining room.

"It's a present. It must be," she said, looking at it in a dazed way. "But I can't think who it could be from."

"A good way to find out would be to open it," remarked Miranda.

Rebecca untied the string and found two small packages inside. She opened the one addressed to her. The package contained a small box and when she lifted the cover, she saw a long chain of delicate, pink coral beads — ending in a cross made of coral rosebuds. A card which read, "Merry Christmas from Mr. Aladdin," lay under the cross.

"Of all things!" exclaimed the aunts, rising in their seats. "Who sent it?"

"Mr. Ladd," said Rebecca under her breath.

"Adam Ladd! Well, I never!" was all Aunt Miranda could say.

There was a letter which read:

Dear Miss Rebecca Rowena,
    My idea of a Christmas present is something entirely unnecessary and

useless. I have always noticed that people love this sort of thing, so I hope
I have not chosen wrong for you and
your friend. You must wear your
chains this afternoon, please, for I am
coming over in my new sleigh to take
you both for a drive. My aunt is delighted with the soap.

Sincerely, your friend,
Adam Ladd

"Well," cried Jane, "isn't that kind of him?
He's very fond of children, Mirandy. Lyddy
Burnham says so. Now eat your breakfast,
Rebecca, and after we've done the dishes you
can run over to Emma's and give her her
chain. Why, what's the matter, child?"

Rebecca's emotions always seemed to be
getting mixed. At this moment, though her
joy was too deep for words, the bread and
butter she was eating almost choked her, and
tears stole down her cheeks.

Mr. Ladd called as he promised, and chat-
ted with the Sawyers as if he had known
them for years. Rebecca sat on a footstool
near the open fire, silent and shy. Her new
dress and the presence of Aunt Miranda
made her so self-conscious that she could not
utter a word.

During the sleigh ride, however, Rebecca found her tongue and chattered like a magpie, and so ended that glorious Christmas Day. For many nights afterward Rebecca went to sleep with the precious coral chain under her pillow, one hand on it to be certain that it was safe.

Soon after Christmas the Simpson family moved away from Riverboro. Rebecca was delighted to be rid of Seesaw, but she missed the companionship of the other children.

The evening before the Simpsons left, Seesaw called at the brick house. When Rebecca answered his knock at the side door, he stammered solemnly, "Can I k-keep company with you when you g-g-row up?"

"Certainly *not*," replied Rebecca, speedily closing the door.

Not long after the Simpsons had departed, Rebecca and Emma Jane were saddened to learn that a church along their route had acquired a magnificent banquet lamp. Abner Simpson had no doubt made another trade.

That winter Dick Carter, Living Perkins, and Huldah Meserve left Riverboro for Wareham Academy. There were few pupils attending the school in the winter, for the younger children often stayed away during the cold weather.

Life, however, could never be dull or lacking in adventure for Rebecca. She made friends everywhere, and snatched up acquaintances at every turn. She would run to the shed door to take the dish to the meat man or fish man, and knew their family histories. She had supper at the houses of children in neighboring towns or even stayed the night. She loved Emma Jane, and liked to talk with Dick Carter, and enjoyed Huldah's sense of fun.

Jeremiah Cobb was probably the only person in Riverboro who had Rebecca's entire confidence; the only one to whom she poured out her hopes, and dreams, and vague ambitions. But there were times when she thought, if only there were somebody who not only loved her but who spoke her language, and understood her vague, mysterious longings! In the bigger world of Wareham she hoped there would be people who thought and dreamed and wondered as she did.

As time passed Rebecca gave up the idea of becoming a painter like her friend Miss Ross. It was too difficult to get instruction in Riverboro and Aunt Miranda did not believe that Rebecca could ever earn a living as an artist. Music, too, was viewed by Miranda as a useless and foolish amusement, though she did allow Rebecca an hour a day to practice on the Sawyers' old piano.

In the next year, Rebecca shot up like a young tree. Once she started to grow, she did it as she did other things — with such energy that Aunt Jane did nothing for months but lengthen skirts and sleeves, and let out waists. When the limit of letting down and piecing together was reached at last, Rebecca's dresses were sent to Sunnybrook Farm to be made over for Jenny.

That year a great sorrow struck the Randalls at Sunnybrook Farm. Mira, the baby of the family, died. Rebecca went home to spend two weeks with her mother and the children.

It was a sorrowful homecoming for her. Mira had been her special charge before Rebecca went to live with her aunts in Riverboro, and the little grave under the willow tree seemed pitiful to her. Her favorite brother John, who had been a close companion, was now living away at their Cousin Ann's house. Even Hannah had changed. She seemed older in some ways than Aunt Jane — soberer and more settled. And the sadness of her mother and the poverty in the little house depressed Rebecca terribly.

To find some comfort she walked through

all the old playgrounds and favorite haunts of her early childhood — all her familiar, secret places. They marked the stages of her childhood, and she looked at them as if from across a great distance. Sunnybrook lay cold, quiet, and covered with snow. There was no water sparkling in the sunshine, no stream dancing over white pebbles on its way to deep pools. Rebecca knelt by the edge and put her ear to the ice. She could hear a faint, tinkling sound. It was all right! Sunnybrook would sing again.

While she walked about on these lonely rambles she kept thinking about her sister. Hannah had never had the chance to be free from the daily care and work of the farm, while she, Rebecca, had enjoyed many advantages. Life at the brick house had not been easy, but there had been many comforts as well; the companionship of other children her own age; and a chance to study and read. All of these things meant a lot to Rebecca and she shed more than one tear before she made up her mind to offer her sister what she wanted to keep so much for herself.

One morning before her visit ended she said to Hannah, "After this term, I'm coming home and let you go away. Aunt Miranda always wanted you, and it's only fair you should have your turn."

Hannah was darning stockings and she snipped off the yarn before she answered. "No thank you, Becky. Mother couldn't do without me, and I hate going to school. I can read and write and do arithmetic as well as anybody now. That's enough for me. I'd die rather than teach school for a living. Our neighbor, Will Melville, is going to lend me his mother's sewing machine, and I'm going to sew petticoats out of the material Aunt Jane sent us. Then there's going to be a singing school and a social circle in Temperance. I shall have a real good time now I'm grown up. I'm not lonesome, Becky," Hannah ended with a blush. "I love this place."

Rebecca saw that Hannah was speaking the truth, but she did not understand her sister's blush till a year or two later.

Rebecca Represents the Family

BEFORE REBECCA ENDED her final school term in Riverboro, an event took place which finally changed Aunt Miranda's opinion of her. That event was the visit of the Reverend and Mrs. Amos Burch, missionaries who had just returned from Syria.

The Aid Society had scheduled its missionary meeting for a Wednesday. When the day dawned raw and blustery, both Miranda and Jane, who had caught colds, decided that they could not leave the house. Since Miranda was an officer of the society, she was worried about being absent from the meeting. At breakfast she decided that Rebecca must go in place of herself and Jane.

"Your Aunt Jane shall write you an excuse from afternoon school," she said. "Reverend Burch, if I remember right, used to know your Grandfather Sawyer, and stayed here

111

once. Maybe he'll look for us there. You must go and represent the family and give him our respects. Be careful how you behave."

Rebecca was quite willing to go, and she thought the idea of representing the family rather exciting.

The meeting was held in the Sunday-school room. Reverend Burch was on the platform when Rebecca entered. There were about a dozen people present. Feeling a little shy and uncomfortable among the adults, Rebecca looked around for a friendly face. When she saw Alice Robinson's mother in one of the side seats near the front, she walked up the aisle and sat down beside her.

"My aunts have bad colds," she said softly. "They sent me to represent the family."

Mrs. Robinson smiled and nodded. "That's Mrs. Burch on the platform with her husband," she whispered to Rebecca.

Mrs. Burch was a slim little woman, dressed in black. She looked so tired that Rebecca's heart went out to her.

"They're poor as can be," whispered Mrs. Robinson, "but if you give 'em anything they'd turn right around and give it to the needy."

The meeting began with a prayer. Then

Reverend Burch asked, "Is there anyone present who can play the organ for us?"

Everybody looked at everybody else, and nobody moved. Then a voice came from the back of the room, "Rebecca, why don't you?" It was Mrs. Cobb. Rebecca was confident about her playing, and went to the organ without any feeling of self-consciousness.

After the hymn, Reverend Burch made his appeal. He asked the members of the Aid Society to help him spread the gospel abroad, and his sermon was filled with stories of life in Syria.

Rebecca sat entranced; she had been given the key to another world. Riverboro and the room faded away. Instead she saw blue skies and burning stars, white turbans and gay colors. Reverend Burch had not said so, but she imagined there were mosques and temples and minarets and datepalms. She came out of her trance only when she was asked to play the organ again.

Later, as the service was coming to an end, Reverend Burch made an announcement. "If any of the sisters will provide accommodations," he said, "Mrs. Burch and I will remain here tonight, and then tomorrow we can hold a parlor meeting. My wife and one of my children will wear the native costume. We will show some examples of Syrian handwork and tell you about our teaching methods with the children. If any member of the congregation offers her hospitality, we will gladly stay and tell you more of the Lord's work."

A pall of silence settled over the little group. Mrs. Burch's thin hands fingered her black silk nervously. "Will no one speak!" thought Rebecca, her heart fluttering with sympathy.

At that moment Mrs. Robinson leaned over and whispered in her ear, "The missionaries always used to be entertained at the brick house. Your grandfather never let them sleep anywhere else when he was alive."

She meant her remark only as a comment on Miranda Sawyer's stinginess, but Rebecca thought it was intended as a suggestion. If it had been the custom, Rebecca decided, her aunts would want her to do the right thing. Delighted at such a pleasant duty, she rose from her seat and said in a clear voice, "My aunts, Miss Miranda and Miss Jane Sawyer, would be very happy to have you visit them at the brick house, just as the ministers always used to do when their father was alive. They sent their respects by me."

Rebecca's manner of delivery was very

impressive. Some of the audience concluded that Miranda Sawyer must be very ill, for what else could cause such an abrupt change of heart?

Reverend Burch bowed courteously and accepted the invitation.

Rebecca sat down again and after a closing prayer and a benediction the meeting ended. In a moment or two, Rebecca went up to Mrs. Burch, who kissed her affectionately. "My dear, how grateful I am that we are going to stay with you. Will half past five be too late for us to come? We have to go to the station for our valise and for our children. We left them there, because we did not know if we would be staying here."

Rebecca said that half past five was the Sawyer's usual supper hour, then she accepted an invitation to drive home with Mrs. Cobb. Rebecca's face was flushed and her lip quivered with excitement. The trip was made almost in silence. The bleak wind and Sarah Cobb's quieting presence calmed her down, and she entered the brick house full of her news.

A Change of Heart

"I T WAS A VERY SMALL MEETING, Aunt Miranda," Rebecca began, "and the missionary and his wife are lovely people. They are coming here to stay all night and tomorrow with you."

"Coming here!" exclaimed Miranda, letting her knitting fall in her lap. "Did they invite themselves?"

"No," Rebecca answered. "I invited them for you. It was this way. . . ."

"Stop your explaining, and tell me first when they'll be here. Right away?"

"No, not for two hours — about half past five."

"Then you can explain, if you can, who gave you any authority to invite strangers to stop here overnight, when you know we ain't had any company for twenty years."

"Don't blame her, Miranda, till you've

116

heard her story," Jane said. "We sent her along to the meeting."

Rebecca began again. "The meeting was a small one. I gave all your messages and everybody was disappointed you couldn't come. Reverend Burch talked beautifully and the singing went real well. Then Reverend Burch said, if any sister would offer hospitality, they would pass the night and have a parlor meeting in Riverboro tomorrow. He waited and waited, and nobody said a word. I was so mortified I didn't know what to do.

"Just then Mrs. Robinson whispered to me that the missionaries always used to stay at the brick house when Grandfather was alive. I thought I ought to invite them, as you weren't there to do it yourself, and you told me to represent the family."

"What did you do — go up and introduce yourself as folks was leaving?"

"No, I stood right up in meeting. I had to. Nobody was speaking up and Reverend Burch's feelings were getting hurt. After I invited them for you, Reverend Burch prayed for Grandfather. He called him a man of God and thanked our Heavenly Father that Grandfather's spirit was still alive in his descendants — that was you — and that the good old house, where so many of the brethren had been cheered and helped, was still open for the stranger and wayfarer."

If Rebecca had plotted for days with the utmost cunning she could not have touched her aunt's soul more effectively. Because of her actions, the Sawyer name had been publicly dignified and praised. Rebecca had conducted herself as a true granddaughter of Deacon Israel Sawyer, and proved that she was not all Randall after all. Miranda was pleased with Rebecca and satisfied with the turn of events, although she did not intend to show it.

"Well, you did only what you was obliged to do, Rebecca," she said. "But why didn't your missionaries come right along with you?"

"They had to go to the station for their luggage and their children."

"Are there children?" Miranda gasped. "How many?"

"I didn't think to ask, but I'll get two rooms ready. If we need more than two I'll take 'em into my bed," said Rebecca, secretly hoping that there would be more. "Now, since you're both half sick, couldn't you trust me just once to get ready for the company? Will you?"

"I believe I will," sighed Miranda reluctantly. "I'll lie down for awhile and see if I can get strength to cook supper. Fix up the two south chambers, Rebecca."

Rebecca, given a free hand for the only time in her life, dashed upstairs like a whirlwind. Every room in the brick house was always kept neat, so she had only to pull up the shades, go over the floors with a broom, and dust the furniture. When she called her aunts at five o'clock, everything was in perfect order.

The Burch family arrived promptly, with only two of their children; eight others had been left with members of the church in Portland. Rebecca guided the two little girls upstairs, took off their wraps, smoothed their hair, and brought them down to supper.

After the meal, Mr. and Mrs. Cobb and Deacon and Mrs. Milliken arrived and everyone went into the parlor.

It was such a pleasant evening! The Burches told strange and marvelous stories about their experiences in Syria. Their two children sang together, and Rebecca, at the request of Mrs. Burch, played the piano with considerable spirit and style.

"That niece of yours is a most remarkable

119

girl," said Reverend Burch after Rebecca had left the room to help the children get ready for bed.

"She seems to be turning out smart enough lately," answered Miranda, "but she's mostly too lively."

"We must remember that it is too little, not too much vitality that makes the greatest trouble in this world," replied Reverend Burch.

Before Miranda could answer, Deacon Milliken spoke up. "Mirandy, do you know who Rebecky reminds me of?"

"I can guess pretty well," she replied.

"Then you've noticed it too! She's so like your father."

"I don't see how you make that out," said Miranda, thoroughly astonished.

"It struck me this afternoon when she got up to give your invitation in meeting. You know his old way of holding his chin up and throwing his head back a little when he got up to say anything? Well, she done the very same thing. There was more than one spoke of it."

The four guests left before nine, and everyone retired for the night.

Rebecca was awake before six the next morning, so full of household cares that sleep was impossible. She went to the window and looked out. It was another dark and stormy day.

"Aunt Jane said she would get up at half past six and have breakfast ready at half past seven," she thought. "They are both so sick with their colds that I think I'll just creep down and start things for a surprise."

Rebecca put on her bathrobe and slippers and stole quietly down the front stairs, carefully closing the kitchen door behind her so that no noise would awaken the rest of the household. For a half hour she was busy getting things ready for seven people's breakfasts, then she went back to her room to dress before calling the children.

The evening before, Jane had felt better than Miranda and had taken over in the kitchen. But in the night she had grown worse. She was unable to leave her bed in the morning. She tossed about with a feverish headache, wondering how her sister could manage without her.

Miranda was wondering this too as she walked stiffly through the dining room, intending to start the breakfast fire and then call Rebecca. She opened the kitchen door and stared about her, wondering whether she had strayed into the wrong house by mistake.

The shades were up, and there was a roaring fire in the stove. The teakettle was singing and bubbling as it sent out a cloud of steam. The coffee was ready and the cold potatoes and corned beef were in the wooden tray, with "Regards of Rebecca" stuck on the chopping knife. The bread was out, the toast rack was out, and the doughnuts were out. The milk was skimmed and the butter had been brought in from the icehouse.

Miranda sank into the kitchen rocker, exclaiming under her breath, "She is the most unusual child! I declare, she is all Sawyer!"

The day and the evening passed with credit to everybody, and that night the Burches left with many regrets. Their children, who swore eternal friendship with Rebecca, were in tears.

It would be pleasant to state that Miranda Sawyer was a changed woman afterward, but that is not the fact. It is true though that she began to take some small secret pride in Rebecca's ability and that she was not quite as severe from that time on.

The Skyline Widens

*T*HE TIME SO LONG and eagerly waited for had come; Rebecca was a student at Wareham. The Academy was an extraordinary experience for her, as much of a change from Riverboro as that village had been from Sunnybrook Farm. Rebecca's intention was to complete the four-year course in three years, as everyone, including Rebecca herself, felt that when she reached seventeen she must be ready to earn her own living and help in the education of her younger brother and her sisters.

Rebecca was to go back and forth to school by railroad every day from September to Christmas, and then board in Wareham during the three coldest winter months.

As for Rebecca's best friend, Emma Jane, her parents had always thought that a year or two in the nearby Edgewood High School would be quite enough education for their daughter, and Emma Jane had readily agreed. If there was one thing she detested it was the learning of lessons. But things looked quite different to her when she started at Edgewood and Rebecca began to go to Wareham. Emma Jane bore the separation from Rebecca for a week, then begged her father to let her change schools. At first Mr. Perkins refused. But when Mrs. Perkins supported her daughter against him, he was forced to give in.

Emma Jane was delirious with joy. Not even the school's difficult entrance examinations discouraged her. She passed in only two out of seven subjects, but cheerfully entered the school on probation.

The village of Wareham was quite lovely, with a broad main street shaded by great maples and elms. It had a drugstore, several different kinds of shops, two churches, and many boardinghouses. But all the town's interests centered about the Academy. Boys and girls from all parts of the county and state, and from all kinds and conditions of homes attended this seat of learning.

Among the students was Huldah Meserve, who had gone to school with Emma Jane and Rebecca in Riverboro. Huldah was a very pretty girl — but quite vain. She had come to

Wareham resolved to have a good time, and her idea of pleasure was to have an ever-changing circle of admirers to fetch and carry for her; to be constantly chattering, teasing, and flirting; and to boast about her conquests to less popular girls. Rebecca and Emma Jane grew weary of listening to her boasting and they avoided her. They would sit at one end of the railway train, going to and from Riverboro, while Huldah and her friends occupied the other.

Among the teachers at Wareham was one who had a strong influence on Rebecca. Miss Emily Maxwell taught English literature and composition. She was the niece of a former governor of Maine and the daughter of a college professor.

"You'll like her; she writes," whispered Huldah to Rebecca the first morning of prayers. "She writes; and I call her stuck-up."

At least one person had seen with his own eyes an essay of Miss Maxwell's published in a magazine. This height of achievement made Rebecca feel rather shy of her, and in the classroom she looked at her teacher with open admiration.

One day, when their first essays were being discussed, Miss Maxwell asked her pupils to bring her some compositions they had written the year before. That way, she would know better what kind of writing her pupils could do. Rebecca lingered after the other students had left and approached the teacher's desk shyly.

"I haven't any compositions here, Miss Maxwell, but I can find one when I go home tonight. They are packed away in a box in the attic."

"Carefully tied with pink and blue ribbons?" asked Miss Maxwell, teasing her.

"No," answered Rebecca, shaking her head decidedly. "I wanted to use ribbons — all the other girls did — but I tied my essays with twine on purpose. The one on solitude I fastened with an old shoelace just to show what I thought of it!"

"Solitude!" laughed Miss Maxwell, raising her eyebrows. "Did you choose your own subject?"

"No. Miss Dearborn thought we were not old enough to find good ones. My compositions were all bad and I can't bear to show them. But I can write poetry easier and better, Miss Maxwell."

"Poetry!" she exclaimed. "Did Miss Dearborn require you to write poetry?"

"Oh, no! I always did, even at the farm. Shall I bring all I have? It isn't much."

"By all means," Miss Maxwell said.

The next day, Rebecca left the book in which she kept copies of her poems at the door of Miss Maxwell's office.

A few days later she saw the book on her teacher's desk and knew that the dreaded moment of criticism had come. She was not surprised to be asked to remain after class.

The room was quiet as Miss Maxwell sat down in the desk next to Rebecca's.

"Did you think these were good?" she asked, giving her the verses.

"Not so very," confessed Rebecca, "but it's hard to tell all by yourself. The Perkinses and the Cobbs always said they were wonderful. But when Mrs. Cobb told me she thought they were better than Henry Wadsworth Longfellow's, I was worried, because I knew that couldn't be true."

This frank remark confirmed Miss Maxwell's opinion of Rebecca as a girl who could hear the truth, and profit by it.

"Well, my child," she said, "your friends were wrong and you were right."

"Then I must give up all hope of ever being a writer!" Rebecca wondered if she could keep the tears back until the interview was over.

"Don't go so fast," interrupted Miss Max-

127

well. "Though your poems don't amount to anything as poetry, they show a good deal of promise in certain directions. You almost never make a mistake in rhyme or meter, and this shows you have a natural ear for poetry. When you grow older, and have a little experience — in fact, when you have something to say — I think you may write very good verse. Poetry needs knowledge and vision, experience and imagination, Rebecca. You haven't the first three yet, but I rather think you have a touch of the last."

"Must I never try any more poetry — not even to amuse myself?"

"Certainly you may. It will help you to write better. For the first composition, I am going to ask all the new students to write a letter giving some description of this town and a hint of the school life."

"Shall I have to be myself?" asked Rebecca.

"What do you mean?"

"A real letter from Rebecca Randall to her sister Hannah at Sunnybrook Farm, or to her Aunt Jane at the brick house, Riverboro, is so dull. If I could make believe I was a different girl altogether, and write to somebody who would be sure to understand everything I said, I could make it much better."

"Very well. I think that's a delightful plan," said Miss Maxwell. "Who will you be?"

"I like heiresses very much," replied Rebecca thoughtfully. "Of course I never knew one, but interesting things are always happening to heiresses. My heiress wouldn't be vain and haughty. She would be noble and generous. She would give up a grand school in Boston because she wanted to come here where her father lived when he was a boy, long before he made his fortune. Her father is dead now and she has a guardian. He is rather old, of course, and sometimes very quiet and grave. But when he is happy he is full of fun, and then Evelyn is not afraid of him. I shall call the girl Evelyn Abercrombie and her guardian's name shall be Mr. Adam Ladd."

"Do you know Mr. Ladd?" asked Miss Maxwell in surprise.

"Yes, he's my very best friend," Rebecca cried delightedly. "Do you know him too?"

"Oh yes. He's a trustee of the school, you know, and often comes here. But if I let you suppose anymore, you will tell me your whole letter and then I shall lose a pleasant surprise."

A Precious Friendship

"*H*ELLO," said Huldah Meserve, peering in at the door of the room Rebecca and Emma Jane shared. The girls were living in Wareham now, for the weather was too bad to travel back and forth each day to Riverboro on the train.

"Can you stop studying a minute and show me your room?" Huldah asked. "None of the other rooms can begin to compare with it! I don't know what gives it that special look. My, haven't you got a lot of new things?"

"Our Christmas presents, you mean," said Emma Jane. "The pillowcases are from Mrs. Cobb, the rug from my cousin in North Riverboro, the scrap basket from Living and Dick, and we gave each other the bureau and cushion covers. The screen is mine from Mr. Ladd."

"Well, you were lucky when you met him. I

wish I could meet somebody like that. I don't see how you got this room when you're only new students," she finished discontentedly.

"We wouldn't have, except that Ruth Berry had to leave school on account of her father's death. The room was empty, and Miss Maxwell asked if we might share it," Emma Jane explained.

"The great and only Max is more stiff and standoffish than ever this year," said Huldah. "I've simply given up trying to please her. She is good to her favorites, but she doesn't pay the least attention to anybody else except to make sarcastic speeches about things that are none of her business. I wanted to tell her yesterday it was her place to teach me English, not manners."

"I wish you wouldn't talk against Miss Maxwell to me," Rebecca said hotly. "You know how I feel."

"I know, but I can't understand how you can bear her."

"I not only bear her, I love her!" exclaimed Rebecca. "I think she's the best teacher that ever lived — "

"Well, don't have a fit! Anyway, I've got something better to think of," said Huldah, tossing her head.

"Isn't this your study hour?" asked Emma Jane, hoping to stop the argument.

"Yes, but I lost my Latin book yesterday. I left it in the hall for half an hour and when I went back, it was gone. I had to go to the principal's office today to report it. Mr. Morrison thinks it will be returned, and lent me another.

"There was a perfectly elegant gentleman in the office — a stranger to me," Huldah continued. "I wish he was a new teacher but no such luck, probably. He was too young to be the father of any of the girls, and too old to be anyone's brother. But he was handsome as a picture. He looked at me a lot while I was in the room. It made me so embarrassed I could hardly answer Mr. Morrison's questions."

"You'll have to wear a mask pretty soon if you're going to have any comfort, Huldah," said Rebecca.

Rebecca's stinging words were said with a laugh. There were times when Huldah couldn't make up her mind whether Rebecca was being witty, or whether she was jealous. Usually Huldah preferred to think it was jealousy and let her remarks pass.

"He wore a cameo scarf pin and a gorgeous ring — a queer kind that wound around and around his finger. Oh, I must run! There's the bell!"

With the mention of the ring, Rebecca became interested in Huldah's conversation. She remembered a certain strange ring that belonged to Mr. Aladdin.

Both Rebecca and Emma Jane felt a mixture of romantic and reverent admiration for Adam Ladd, and they felt the liveliest gratitude for his beautiful gifts every Christmas. Emma Jane had seen him only twice, but he had called several times at the brick house. It was Rebecca who always wrote him thank you notes for his gifts, taking pains to make Emma Jane's letter quite different from her own.

Now, as Rebecca hurried off to class, she wondered if Huldah's stranger was Mr. Aladdin and whether he would come to see her.

Later that afternoon, Rebecca was free to enjoy something she looked forward to the entire week. Each Friday after school she took the path through the pine woods at the back of the academy that led into the village street where Miss Maxwell lived. Here in her teacher's sitting room, which was lined with books, she could browse happily until it was time to meet Emma Jane at the station and take the train to Riverboro for the weekend.

She had been reading for half an hour when she glanced out of the window and saw two figures coming out of the woods along the path. The bright red hair under the fashionable hat could belong only to Huldah, and her companion was surely Mr. Aladdin.

Rebecca slipped from her place by the window to the rug before the fire, and leaned her head on the seat of the great easy chair. She was frightened by the strange emotion she felt, and at the suddenness with which it had come on. It was an entirely new sensation. She felt as if she could not bear to share Mr. Aladdin's friendship with the pretty Huldah. She had willingly shared his friendship with Emma Jane, for she realized that her friend held only a secondary place in Mr. Aladdin's regard. Now, Rebecca wondered, who was she herself, to hope that she could hold first place in his affections?

The door opened softly and somebody looked in and said, "Miss Maxwell told me I should find Miss Rebecca Randall here."

Rebecca started at the words and sprang to her feet. "Mr. Aladdin! I knew you were in Wareham, and I was afraid you wouldn't have time to come and see us."

"Who is 'us'? The aunts are not here, are they? Oh, you mean the rich blacksmith's daughter, whose name I can never remember. Is she here?"

"Yes, she's my roommate," answered Rebecca.

"Well, Rebecca," Adam said smiling, "I'm on my way to a meeting of railway directors in Portland, tomorrow, and I always take the opportunity to stop by the school and give my advice concerning its affairs."

"It seems funny for you to be a school trustee," said Rebecca thoughtfully. "I can't seem to make it fit."

"You are a remarkably wise young person and I quite agree with you," he answered. "The fact is, I accepted the trusteeship in memory of my mother, whose years spent here as a student were her last happy ones."

"That was a long time ago!"

"Let me see. I am thirty-two — only thirty-two despite a few gray hairs — my mother was married a month after she graduated and she died when I was ten. Yes, it is a long way back to my mother's time here. Would you like to see a picture of my mother, Rebecca?"

Rebecca took the leather case he handed her and opened it. She saw a young, sensitive face, so trusting and hopeful it went straight to her heart.

"Oh, what a sweet face!" she whispered softly.

"She had to bear all sorts of storms," said Adam gravely. "I was only a child and could do nothing to protect her from trouble. Now I have success and money and power, all that would have kept her alive and happy, and it is too late. She died for lack of love and care and I can never forget it. Sometimes all that I have seems useless, since I cannot share it with her!"

This was a new Mr. Aladdin, and Rebecca understood the tired look in his eyes that showed now and then under all his gay talk and laughter.

"I'm so glad I know," she said, "and so glad I could see her just as she was when she tied that white muslin hat under her chin. She must have been happy then! I wish she could have remained so, and could have lived to see you grow up strong and good. My mother is always sad and busy, but once when she looked at John, I heard her say, 'He makes up for everything.' That's what your mother would have thought about you if she had lived — and perhaps she does as it is."

"You are a comforting little person, Rebecca," said Adam, rising from his chair and taking her hands in his.

He looked at her suddenly as if he was seeing her for the first time. "Why, little Rose-Red Snow-White is making way for a new girl! She is so tall that she reaches almost to my shoulder. This will never do! How will Mr. Aladdin get on without his comforting little friend? He doesn't like grown-up young ladies in long trains and wonderful fine clothes. They frighten and bore him!"

"Oh, Mr. Aladdin!" Rebecca cried eagerly, taking his joke quite seriously, "I am not fifteen yet, and it will be three years before I'm a young lady. Please don't give me up until you have to!"

"I won't. I promise you that," said Adam.

Misfortunes

*T*HE FIRST HAPPPY YEAR at Wareham was over and gone. Rebecca studied during the summer vacation and returned to school in the autumn. Though she was not an outstanding student, she had done well in some subjects and brilliantly in others, so that she had a respectable average. Even if she didn't know the answer to a question, she could usually offer some original ideas; though not always correct, they were usually unique and sometimes amusing.

"She can be perfectly ignorant of a subject," Miss Maxwell explained to Adam Ladd, "but entirely intelligent the moment she has a clue. Most of the other girls are full of information and as stupid as sheep."

During the first year, Rebecca had settled quietly into the routine of the school. Because she had extra classes and homework, she had less free time than the other students to enjoy the social side of school life. Nevertheless, by the spring of her second year, she had become the most popular figure in the school. There was little surprise when she was unanimously elected assistant editor of the Wareham *School Pilot* — the first girl to have that position.

Despite her success at school, Rebecca was full of small anxieties and fears. Things were not going well at the brick house or at Sunnybrook Farm.

It seemed to her that Aunt Miranda had never been so harsh and critical. One Saturday, matters came to a head. Rebecca, in a flood of tears, blurted out her misery to Aunt Jane.

"I never could stand her continual scoldings, and nothing I do suits Aunt Miranda. She says it will take me my whole life to get the Randall out of me, and I'm not sure that I want it all out. So there we are!"

Aunt Jane, tried to soothe her. "You must be patient," she said, wiping the tears from her own eyes. "I haven't told you, because I didn't think it was fair to trouble you when you were studying so hard. Your Aunt Miranda isn't well. Her health's failing and that's what makes her so difficult. She has other troubles, too, that I can't speak about, but if you're not kind to her now, child, you'll be dreadfully sorry someday."

All the temper faded from Rebecca, and she stopped crying. "Oh! The poor dear. I won't let anything she says bother me now. She asked me to make her some milk toast and I was dreading to take it to her. But this makes everything different. Thank you for telling me, Aunt Jane, and don't worry. Perhaps she isn't as sick as you think."

When Rebecca carried the toast to her aunt a little later, there was a fringed napkin and a sprig of geranium lying on the tray.

"Now, Aunt Miranda," she said cheerily, "I hope you'll like this. It's not Randall, but Sawyer milk toast."

"You've tried all kinds on me, one time and another," Miranda answered. "This does taste good, but I wish you hadn't wasted that nice geranium."

"It isn't wasted," said Rebecca, "if it brightens somebody's supper."

The mysterious trouble that Jane had mentioned was very real, but it was held in strict secrecy. Years before, twenty-five hundred dollars from the small Sawyer estate had been invested in the business of a friend of their father's. The investment had given the two women a regular annual income of one hundred dollars. Now, suddenly, the firm had gone bankrupt, and the Sawyer money had been swept away with everything else.

The loss of one hundred dollars a year was not a great amount, but it made all the difference between comfort and self-denial to the two old spinsters. Their manner of life had been so careful that it was difficult to economize any further, and the blow had fallen just when Rebecca's school and boarding expenses had to be paid.

"Can we possibly go on paying for it? Won't we have to give up and tell her why?" Jane asked Miranda tearfully.

"We took Rebecca away from her mother and offered her an education. We've got to keep our word," Miranda said in a grim voice. "She's Aurelia's only hope, to my way of thinking. Hannah's beau takes all *her* time and thought, and John, instead of farming, thinks he must be a doctor. No, Jane, we'll skimp and do without, and plan to git along somehow."

Rebecca, who knew nothing of her aunts' business affairs, merely saw them carry economy to its very extreme. She had to bear with Miranda's gloomy and uncompromising manner, but her aunt never accused her of being a burden. Rebecca's share of the Sawyers' economy consisted only in wearing her old clothes without any apparent hope of a change.

There was, however, no concealing the state of things at Sunnybrook. That year the potato crop had failed; there were few apples; and the hay had been poor. In addition, Rebecca's mother was suffering with dizzy spells; Mark had broken his ankle; and the time for paying the interest on the mortgage had come and gone. For the first time in fourteen years, the Randalls could not raise the required forty-eight dollars. The only bright spot in the year was Hannah's engagement to Will Melville, the young farmer whose land adjoined Sunnybrook.

Shortly before her engagement, Hannah spent a week at the brick house. Miranda's impression of her, told in privacy to Jane, was that Hannah was a selfish girl who would never help the other members of her family, no matter how well she did herself.

"I was glad to see her face turned toward Temperance," Miranda admitted. "If that mortgage is ever cleared from the farm, it won't be Hannah that'll do it. It'll be Rebecca or me!"

Mr. Aladdin Rubs His Lamp

"*Y*OUR ESTEEMED CONTRIBUTION, 'Wareham Wildflowers' has been accepted for *The Pilot*, Miss Perkins," said Rebecca entering the room, where Emma Jane was darning stockings.

"You are joking, Becky!" Emma Jane exclaimed, looking up from her work.

"Not a bit. The senior editor read it and thought it highly instructive. It will appear in the next issue."

"Rebecca," said Emma Jane in a most dramatic voice, "I don't know if I shall be able to bear it. If anything happens to me, I ask you solemnly to bury that issue of *The Pilot* with me."

Rebecca did not seem to think that Emma Jane's reaction was unusual, for she replied, "That's just the way I felt at first. Even now, whenever I read over my contributions in back issues of *The Pilot*, I almost burst with pleasure. It's not that they are good either, for they look worse to me every time I read them."

"If we could live together in some little house when we get older," mused Emma Jane, "I would do the housework and cooking, and you needn't do anything but write. It would be perfectly elegant!"

"I'd like nothing better, but I promised to keep house for John," replied Rebecca.

"He won't have a house for a good many years, will he?"

"No," sighed Rebecca, flinging herself down by the table and resting her head on her hand. "Not unless we can pay off that detestable mortgage. And that day seems further off than ever."

She pulled a piece of paper toward her, and scribbled on it idly for a moment. Then she read aloud:

"Will you pay a little faster?" said the
    mortgage to the farm;
"I confess I'm very tired of this place."
"The weariness is mutual," Rebecca Ran-
    dall cried;
"I would I'd never gazed upon your face!"

"A bank note has a 'face,'" observed Emma Jane, who was gifted in arithmetic. "I didn't know that a mortgage had."

"Our mortgage has," said Rebecca revengefully. "I should know the fiend even if I met him in the dark."

Lately Adam Ladd had been going to Temperance on business connected with building the new branch line of the local railroad. While he was there he learned a bit about conditions at Sunnybrook. The information helped him understand why Rebecca did not seem her usual cheerful self the next time he saw her in Wareham. He noticed that she looked pale and thin, though she was holding to her heavy schedule of work. She was wearing a black cashmere dress that had been Aunt Jane's second best. As always, the lines of her trim figure and the rare coloring of her skin and hair and eyes overpowered her shabby clothing.

Adam looked at her so intently that Rebecca put her hands over her face and laughed. "I know what you are thinking, Mr. Aladdin," she said. "My dress is an inch longer than last year and my hair is different. But sixteen is a month off yet and you promised not to give me up until my dress trails the floor. If you don't like me to grow old, why don't you grow young? Then we can meet halfway. Now that I think about it," she continued, "that's just what you've been doing all along. When you bought the soap, I thought you were Grandfather Sawyer's age. When you visited at the brick house you seemed like my father; but when you showed me your mother's picture, I felt as if you were my brother John."

Adam smiled. "Don't go so swiftly that you become my grandmother before I really need one," he answered. "You are studying too hard, Miss Rebecca Rowena!"

"Just a little," she confessed. "But vacation comes soon, you know."

"And are you going to have a good rest and try to recover your sunny spirits? They are really worth preserving."

A shadow crept over Rebecca's face and her eyes filled with tears. "Don't be kind, Mr. Aladdin, I can't bear it — it's — it's not one of my sunny days!" She ran in at the school gate, and disappeared with a farewell wave of her hand.

Adam Ladd walked on to the principal's office in a thoughtful mood. The Wareham Academy was just fifty years old, and he had already given them several generous anniversary gifts. After his talk with Rebecca he decided to do more. He would ask the principal, Mr. Morrison, to arrange a contest in which he would offer two cash prizes to students in the upper classes for the best original English composition. He was hoping that Rebecca would be able to win one of the prizes for he knew how much she needed the money.

After Adam had made arrangements for the contest with Mr. Morrison, he called on Miss Maxwell. He needed her help with another idea that was taking shape in his mind.

He had scarcely greeted her when he said, "Miss Maxwell, doesn't it strike you that Rebecca looks wretchedly tired?"

"She does indeed. I was wondering if I could take her away with me," replied Miss Maxwell. "I always go South for the spring vacation, traveling by sea and relaxing in some quiet spot along the coast. I should like nothing better than to have Rebecca for a companion."

"The very thing!" Adam agreed. The two sat down and between them settled all the details for the spring trip.

The journey southward, the ocean, the feeling of freedom, delighted and thrilled Rebecca. In three days she was not only herself again, but a new self. She had always been trying to make the outward world match her inward dreams. Now, all at once, life had grown rich and sweet, wide and full. But even during these golden days the prize essay was very much on Rebecca's mind. Secretly she thought she could never be happy unless she won it. She cared, of course, for the value of it, but mostly she wanted to please Mr. Aladdin.

"If I ever succeed in choosing a subject, may I ask if you think I can write well on it?" she said to Miss Maxwell. "I know I must work on my own after that, never reading the essay to you, or talking about it."

Miss Maxwell and Rebecca had been sitting in a stretch of wood by the sea since breakfast. They would bask on the warm white sand for awhile, then return to the shade of the trees when the sun grew too hot. Each time, Rebecca would lovingly open and shut her new rose-colored parasol, a vacation gift from Mr. Ladd.

"Have you decided on anything yet?" Miss Maxwell asked.

"No," Rebecca answered, "I pick a new subject every night. In Wareham, I didn't have a single thought. Now I have a new one every minute. I should try and write while I am so happy and free and rested. Oh, Miss Maxwell, I am so afraid I shall never get education enough to make a good writer."

"You would do better to worry about many other things connected with writing," Miss Maxwell said. "Be afraid, for instance, that you won't understand human nature; that you won't see the beauty of the world around you; that you may lack sympathy for others — a thousand things, every one of them as important to the writer as knowledge that is found in books. Aesop was a Greek slave who could not even write down his wonderful fables, yet all the world reads them."

"I didn't know that," said Rebecca, with wonder. "I didn't know anything until I met you!"

"You will have only a high school course when you finish at Wareham, but the most famous universities do not always succeed in making men and women."

"Mr. Ladd says that you are almost wasted on Wareham," said Rebecca thoughtfully.

"He is wrong. My talent is not a great one, but no talent is wholly wasted unless its owner chooses to hide it. Remember that of your gifts, Rebecca. You may not gain great fame, but you may cheer, console, or inspire

149

someone, when and where you least expect it."

"Did you ever hear of 'The Rose of Joy'?" asked Rebecca, after a long silence.

"Yes, of course, where did you see it?"

"On the outside of a book in the library."

"I saw it on the inside of a book in the library." Miss Maxwell smiled. "It is in an essay by Ralph Waldo Emerson, but I'm afraid you haven't quite grown up to it, Rebceca, and it is difficult to explain."

"Oh, try me, Miss Maxwell!" pleaded Rebecca. "Perhaps by thinking hard I can guess a little bit what it means."

"I'll try to quote it," Miss Maxwell said. " 'In the actual world — this painful kingdom of time and chance — are Care, Canker, and Sorrow. With thought, with the Ideal, is immortal hilarity — the rose of Joy; round it all the Muses sing.' "

Rebecca repeated the quote. Then she said, "I don't want to be conceited, but I believe I do understand it, Miss Maxwell. Not altogether, perhaps, because it is puzzling and difficult, but a little. I've decided my essay is going to be called 'The Rose of Joy.' Now I'm going to give you the fir pillow so that you can sleep and I am going down on the shore to write."

A Fairy Story

"*The* rose of joy!" The magic of the title quickened Rebecca's imagination — partly, perhaps, because of the lovely rose parasol. Rebecca opened the brightly colored sunshade and set it beside her on the beach. How she loved the warm, rosy glow it made around her as she bent over her writing pad. And how like Mr. Aladdin, she thought, to have picked a gift so close to her heart. It reminded her of the pink parasol of her childhood. That parasol had come from Paris, France, from another dear friend, and had stood for the larger world beyond Riverboro, and even Wareham.

Rebecca laughed a little, remembering how she had tried to discipline herself once by throwing her dearest possession down the well at the brick house. She knew now that "discipline" meant something quite different. It meant, not foolish sacrifice, but training yourself — like training yourself to write. Writing was a kind of discipline. It was also a way of sharing your best thoughts with other people. Oh, I want to write really well, she thought. I want my essay to be the finest thing I've ever written.

But first, she decided, she wanted to write something that would tell Miss Maxwell and perhaps Mr. Aladdin, too, how grateful she felt for all they had done for her. Letters and thank you's weren't enough. She would write — a story.

That evening Rebecca handed Emily Maxwell her story, just as she was going to her room for the night. Miss Maxwell read it with tears in her eyes. Then she sent it to Adam Ladd, knowing he had earned a share in it, and that he deserved a glimpse of Rebecca's budding talent, as well as of her grateful young heart.

A FAIRY STORY

There was once a tired and rather poverty-stricken princess who dwelt in a cottage on the great highway between two cities. She was not as unhappy as thousands of others; indeed, she had much to be grateful for, but the life she lived and the work she did were full hard for one who was fashioned slenderly.

Now the cottage stood by the edge of a great green forest where the wind was always singing in the branches and the sunshine filtering through the leaves.

And one day when the princess was sitting by the wayside quite spent by her labor in the fields, she saw a golden chariot rolling down the king's highway, and in it a person who could be none other than somebody's fairy godmother on her way to the court. The chariot halted at her door, and though the princess had read of such beneficent personages, she never dreamed for an instant that one of them could ever alight at her cottage.

"If you are tired, poor little Princess, why do you not go into the cool green forest and rest?" asked the fairy godmother.

"Because I have no time," she answered. "I must go back to my plough."

"Is that your plough leaning by the tree, and is it not too heavy?"

"It is heavy," answered the princess, "but I love to turn the hard earth into soft furrows and know that I am making good soil wherein seeds may grow. When I feel the weight too much, I try to think of the harvest."

The next morning a strong man knocked at the cottage door, and doffing his hat to the princess said: "A golden chariot passed me yesterday, and one within it flung me a purse of ducats, saying: 'Go out into the king's highway and search until you find a cottage and a heavy plough leaning against a tree near by. Enter and say to the princess whom you will find there: "I will guide the plough and you must go and rest, or walk in the cool green forest; for this is the command of your fairy godmother." ' "

And the same thing happened every day, and every day the tired princess walked in the green wood. Many times she caught the glitter of the chariot and ran onto the highway to give thanks to the fairy godmother; but she was never fleet enough to reach the spot. She could only stand with eager eyes and longing heart as the chariot passed by. Yet she never failed to catch a smile, and sometimes a word or two floated back to her, words that sounded like: "I would not be thanked. We are all children of the same king, and I am only his messenger."

Now as the princess walked daily in the green forest, hearing the wind singing in the branches and seeing the sunlight filter through the latticework of green leaves, there came unto her thoughts that had lain asleep in the stifling air of the cottage and the weariness of guiding the plough. And by and by she took a needle from her girdle and pricked the thoughts on the leaves of the trees and sent them into the air to float hither and thither. And it came to pass that people began to pick them up, and holding them against the sun, to read what was written on them, and this was because the simple little words on the leaves were only, after all, a part of one of the king's messages, such as the fairy godmother dropped continually from her golden chariot.

But the miracle of the story lies deeper than all this.

Whenever the princess pricked the words upon the leaves she added a new thought of her fairy godmother, and folding it close within, sent the leaf out on the breeze to float hither and thither and fall where it would. And many other little princesses felt the same impulse and did the same thing. And as nothing is ever lost in the king's dominion, so these thoughts and wishes and hopes, being full of love and gratitude, had no power to die, but lived on. They cannot be seen, our vision is too weak; nor heard, our hearing is too dull; but they can sometimes be felt, and we know not what force is stirring our hearts to nobler aims.

The end of the story is not come, but it may be that some day when the fairy godmother has a message to deliver in person straight to the king, he will say: "Your face I know; your voice, your thoughts, and your heart. I have heard the rumble of your chariot wheels on the great highway, and I knew that you were on the king's business. Here in my hand is a sheaf of messages from every quarter of my kingdom. They were delivered by weary and footsore travelers, who said that they could never have reached the gate in safety had it not been for your help and inspiration. Read them, that you may know when and where and how you sped the king's service."

And when the fairy godmother reads them, it may be that sweet odors will rise from the pages, and half-forgotten memories will stir the air; but in the gladness of the moment nothing will be half so lovely as the voice of the king when he said: "Read, and know how you sped the king's service."

Rebecca Rowena Randall

Graduation Day

A YEAR HAD PASSED since Adam Ladd's essay prizes had been awarded to Rebecca and a boy in the senior class. The awards committee of three ministers and three deacons had made the decision. Adam Ladd had given each of the winners fifty dollars. The day Rebecca received her prize, she sent the money off to Sunnybrook to pay the interest on the mortgage. And that spring the Randall family had a second reason to celebrate — Hannah and Will Melville were married.

The months had come and gone, and now the great day dawned for Rebecca — the day to which she had been looking forward for many years — graduation day.

The little town of Wareham was shaken to its very center on this day of days. Mothers, fathers, close and distant relatives of students had been arriving on the train and driving into town since breakfast time. Old pupils, married and single, with and without families, streamed back to the old village. The two livery stables were crowded, and buggies and wagons were drawn up along the sides of the shady roads, the horses switching their tails in idleness. The streets were filled with people wearing their best clothes.

The dormitory of the academy buzzed with excitement as the girls helped each other into their long, snowy white dresses.

For awhile it had looked as though Rebecca would not have a graduation dress at all. Then she and Emma Jane had found several pieces of white cheesecloth in the Perkins' attic and decided that it would do if the material was decorated with embroidery. In order to finish the sewing in time, the dress was given out in sections — the sash to Hannah, the bodice and sleeves to Mrs. Cobb, and the skirt to Aunt Jane. The delicate, loving stitches that they sewed into the cheap material turned the dress into a gown of unexpected loveliness.

As the two girls waited in their room, Emma Jane fought back her tears. She kept thinking that this was the last day Rebecca would share this room with her. It seemed like the beginning of the end to her. The day before, Mr. Morrison had told Rebecca of two teaching jobs for which he wanted to recommend her. One was a boarding school in Augusta, where she would play piano for singing and gymnastics, and also direct the piano practice of the younger girls. The other opportunity was as an assistant in the Edgewood High School. Both positions paid very little money, but the one in Augusta included educational advantages that Miss Maxwell thought might be valuable to Rebecca's future.

As the last moments ticked away, the girls' excitement could hardly be contained. When the bell rang through the corridors signaling that the class should proceed to the church for the exercises, Rebecca stood motionless and speechless at the window.

"Emmie," she said. "Do you remember in *The Mill on the Floss* when Maggie Tulliver closed the golden gates of childhood behind her? I'm doing that now, and I can't tell whether I am glad or sorry."

"I shouldn't care so much," said Emma Jane, "if only you and I were on the same side of the gate, but we shan't be, I know we shan't!"

"Emmie, don't you dare cry. I'm just on

the brink myself! If only you were graduating with me — that's my only sorrow! Hug me for luck, dear Emmie, a careful hug, though. Remember the delicate cheesecloth!"

Ten minutes later Adam Ladd, who had just arrived from Portland, came into the main street to watch the graduation procession. Instead of marching two by two from the academy to the church, Rebecca's class had decided to ride there. A hay cart, drawn by two white horses, had been decorated with green vines and bunches of long-stemmed field daisies — the class flower. Every inch of the cart, even the horses' reins and the spokes of the wheels, was entwined with yellow and white flowers. The twelve girls in the class rode in the cart, while the ten boys marched on either side, wearing daisies in their buttonholes.

Adam watched Rebecca, then turned with the crowd and walked toward the church.

From her seat on the stage of the old meeting house, Rebecca could see Hannah and Will, John and Cousin Ann, and Mr. and Mrs. Cobb. She felt a sudden loneliness at the absence of her mother, though she had known there was no possibility of her coming. Mrs. Randall had no money to spare for the journey or for special clothes.

There were other Riverboro faces that Rebecca could pick out in the audience, but where was Aunt Jane? She knew that Aunt Miranda would not be able to come.

The whole morning passed like a series of magic lantern pictures, crossing and recrossing her field of vision. She sang, she read a Latin prayer, she recited the class poem, "Makers of Tomorrow," and she received her diploma.

Then it was over. After the crowd had thinned out a little, Adam Ladd made his way toward the platform.

Rebecca turned from speaking to a group of classmates and met him in the aisle. "Oh, Mr. Aladdin, I am so glad you could come! Tell me, are you pleased with your protégée?"

"Delighted," he said. "I am glad I met the child, proud I know the girl, and eager to meet the woman!"

Sharing and Caring

*B*EFORE REBECCA could find words to answer Adam Ladd, Mr. and Mrs. Cobb approached and she introduced them.

"Where is Aunt Jane?" she asked, putting an arm around each of her dear friends.

"I'm sorry, lovey, but we've got bad news for you."

"Is Aunt Miranda worse? She is. I can see it by your faces." The color faded from Rebecca's cheeks.

"She had a stroke yesterday morning," Mrs. Cobb explained. "Jane said you wasn't to know anything about it till the exercises was all over, and we promised to keep it secret till then."

"I'll go right home with you, Aunt Sarah. I must run and tell Miss Maxwell. I was going to her family's home in Brunswick with her tomorrow. Poor Aunt Miranda! And I have been so happy."

"There ain't no harm in being happy, lovey. That's what Miranda and Jane wanted for you."

"I'll pack your trunk for you, Becky, and attend to the room," said Emma Jane, who had just come up and heard the sad news from the brick house.

Rebecca did not see Aunt Miranda till she had been at the brick house for several days. Miranda refused to have anyone but Jane in the room, but her door was always ajar, and Jane thought that she liked to hear Rebecca's quick, light step. Miranda's mind was perfectly clear, and she could speak slowly, but she could not move.

At last there came a morning when she asked to see her niece. Rebecca pushed open the door into the dim sickroom, and stood with the sunlight behind her. Miranda's pale face looked haggard on the pillow, and her body was pitifully still under the spread.

"Let me look at ye," she said. "Come closer. What dress are ye wearing?"

"My blue calico," Rebecca whispered.

"Is your cashmere holding its color?"

"Yes, Aunt Miranda."

"I was dreadful ashamed to have you graduate in cheesecloth, Rebecca, but I couldn't help it. You'll hear the reason some time. Was you a laughingstock!"

"Oh, no!" Rebecca cried. "Ever so many people said my dress was the very prettiest. You're not to be anxious about anything. Here I am all grown up and graduated and good positions offered me already. If you want me near, I'll take the Edgewood school. If you get better, then I'll go to Augusta — that's a hundred dollars more, with music lessons and other things besides."

"You listen to me," Miranda said in a shaky voice. "Take the best place, regardless of my sickness."

She stopped abruptly, having talked more than she had for weeks. Rebecca stole out of the room to cry by herself, and wish her aunt's old age didn't have to be so hard.

The days went by and Miranda grew stronger. Little by little hope returned to the brick house. Aunt Jane began to help Rebecca put her clothes in order so that she might be ready to go to Brunswick when the doctor pronounced Miranda well enough.

At length the day came when Rebecca felt free to leave. Abijah Flagg was waiting at the door to take her to the station when a telegram came from Hannah: "Come at once. Mother has had a bad accident."

In less than an hour Rebecca was on her way to Sunnybrook, her heart beating with fear.

She found that her mother was conscious and not in serious danger. Her right knee was fractured and her back injured. Mrs. Randall had been working in the haymow in the barn when she had become faint and slipped. As soon as Rebecca had a moment, she wrote these details to Aunt Jane.

"Aurelia was born unfortunate," murmured Miranda, who was able to sit up on the day the letter arrived. "I suppose Rebecca'll have to nurse her instead of earning a good income somewhere else."

"She has a duty to her family," said Aunt Jane. "I hope she'll always remember that."

"Nobody remembers anything they ought to at seventeen," responded Miranda. "Now that I'm strong enough, there's things we ought to talk over, Jane. We've discussed them before, but let's settle them."

"Of course, Miranda."

"I don't want Rebecca to know I've willed her the brick house. She won't get it till I'm gone, and I want to take my time about dying and not be hurried off by them that's going to profit by it. I don't want to be thanked, neither. I know how much she likes you, and she'll want you to have a home here as long as you live, but I've written that down in my will, anyway. I wasn't going to have the man Rebecca picks for a husband turning you out of doors. Now, if you'll draw down the curtain I'll try to sleep."

Good-bye to Sunnybrook

*T*WO MONTHS had gone by — two months of steady, tiring work for Rebecca — cooking, washing, ironing, mending, and caring for her mother and the three children. Many nights she watched by her mother's bedside, soothing and nursing her. Now, at last she and the family could breathe more freely, for their mother was no longer in pain.

No girl of seventeen can go through such an ordeal and come out unchanged. No girl of Rebecca's character could go through such an experience without some inner rebellion.

These thoughts were in Mrs. Randall's mind one October morning when Rebecca came into her room with her arms full of goldenrod and flaming autumn leaves.

In the years when her children were all young, household cares and anxieties had absorbed all Mrs. Randall's attention. Then Rebecca had gone away. Now, because of her accident, she'd had time to study and get to know her daughter. She was delighted with the person Rebecca had become.

"Just a hint of fall, Mother," Rebecca said, slipping the stem of a gorgeous red and yellow sapling between the mattress and the foot of her mother's bed. Isn't it lovely? I wish I could take some to poor Aunt Miranda today! There are never any flowers in the brick house when I'm away."

Mrs. Randall looked at her tall, young daughter, and suddenly covered her eyes. "I can't bear it! I am chained to this bed, keeping you from everything you want to do. It's all wasted! All my saving and doing without. All your hard study. All Mirandy's expense. Everything that we thought was going to be the making of you!"

"Mother, don't talk like that!" exclaimed Rebecca. "Why, I'm only a little past seventeen! This is just the beginning for me.

"Do you remember the young tree that John planted? We had a dry summer and a cold winter and it didn't grow a bit, for all we did for it. Then there was a good year and it put out roots and made up for lost time. Well, I'll be like that. Don't go believing my day is over. It's just beginning!"

"You put on a brave face," sobbed Mrs. Randall, "but you can't deceive me. You will never get a chance to see your friends here. You're nothing but a drudge!"

"A drudge! Why, Mother, when you were seventeen, wasn't it good just to be alive? Have you forgotten?"

"No," said Aurelia, "but I don't think I was ever as alive as you are."

"I often think," Rebecca said, walking over to the window and looking out at the trees, "how dreadful it would be if I had never been born. If you had had Hannah, and then instead of me, John and Jenny and the others, but no Rebecca. Mother, it means everything just to be alive. Oh, look! Will is coming up the lane. I'll see if he has any mail."

Hannah's husband, Will Melville, drove his team of horses up to the house, tossed a letter to Rebecca, and continued on to the barn. Rebecca opened the envelope and read the brief message to her mother.

Your Aunt Miranda died an hour ago. Come at once. I shall not have the funeral till you are here. Miranda died very suddenly and without any pain.
                                    Aunt Jane

Rebecca burst into tears. "Poor, poor Aunt Miranda! She is gone and she didn't take much pleasure in life. I wish I could have said good-bye to her!"

"You must get ready right away," said Mrs. Randall. "Your aunts have done everything in the world for you. Jenny can manage and I'll ask Hannah to come over once a day. I'd give a good deal if I could go to Mirandy's funeral," she added, breaking down and weeping bitterly.

Rebecca had only an hour to catch the train. She flew down the hill to get a last pail of spring water. As she lifted the bucket from the depths and looked out over the glowing beauty of the autumn landscape, she caught her breath. "The time has come!" she thought. "I am saying good-bye to Sunnybrook and to my childhood. Good-bye, dear brook and hills and meadows. We must wish each other joy."

Will Melville drove Rebecca to the new railway station in Temperance. "Cheer up, Becky!" he said, before he drove off. "We'll take care of your mother. She'll be sitting up when you come back. Things will never be as bad again as they have been this last year — that's what Hannah and I think."

Adam Ladd was at the railway office in Temperance when they arrived. He came up to Rebecca as she waited on the station platform.

"You're sad," he said, taking her hand. He thought her sadness was connected with affairs at Sunnybrook. He hadn't seen Rebecca since her graduation two months before. When he realized that her grief was over her aunt's death, he expressed his sympathy. And though he couldn't accompany her to Riverboro, he asked if he might visit her there soon.

As Adam put Rebecca on the train, he thought to himself that in her sad dignity she was more beautiful than he had ever seen her.

Aunt Miranda's Apology

REBECCA GOT OFF the train in Maplewood and hurried to the post office to take the stage. She was overjoyed to see Mr. Cobb waiting for her.

"I knew you wouldn't let the grass grow under your feet when you got Aunt Jane's letter, so I took over from the regular driver. Here I be just as I was years ago. Will you sit up in front with me?"

Rebecca hugged the old man, who had been her first friend in Riverboro. "Oh, Uncle Jerry! Dear Uncle Jerry! It was all so long ago and so much has happened."

"There, there, lovey," the old man whispered comfortingly. "We'll talk things over as we go along the road and maybe they won't look so bad."

Every mile of the way was familiar to Rebecca. She kept looking back to that day, long ago, when she sat on the box seat for the first time, her legs too short to reach the footboard. She could smell the bouquet of lilacs, see the pink parasol and feel the stiffness of her starched cotton dress.

When the Perkins' roof came in sight, Rebecca saw a white cloth fluttering from the attic windows. She recognized Emma Jane's thoughtful message, a silent welcome at the moment the Riverboro chimneys rose into view.

The brick house came next, looking just as it had that first day. There were the rolling meadows, the stately elms and glowing maples, the garden beds bright with asters and hollyhocks. Only now the window blinds were drawn, and there was a scarf of black crepe tied on the brass knocker of the brown-painted door.

"Don't turn in at the drive, Uncle Jerry. Drop me in the road and I'll go up the path."

At the sound of the approaching stage, the house door had opened, and Jane had come out on the stone steps. Rebecca ran up the walk holding out her arms to her old aunt.

"Rebecca," she said, raising her head, "she was a good woman. She had a quick temper and a sharp tongue, but she wanted to do right, and she did it as she saw it. She never said so, but I'm sure she was sorry for every hard word she ever spoke to you. She didn't take them back in life, but she acted so that you'd know her feelings when she was gone."

"I told her before I left that she'd been the making of me." Rebecca's voice was shaking.

"She wasn't that," Jane said. "God made you in the first place, and you've done considerable to help Him along. But Miranda gave you the means to work with, and that's a lot, especially when a person gives up her own luxuries and pleasures to do it. She didn't want you to know while she lived, but your Aunt Mirandy's willed all this to you — the brick house, and the buildings and furniture, and the land all around the house."

Rebecca pulled off her hat and buried her face in her hands. After a moment's silence, she said, "Let me go in alone. I want to talk to her; I want to thank her. I feel as if I could make her hear and feel and understand!"

Ten minutes later Rebecca came out of the house. She stood in the quiet doorway, shaded by the overhanging elms. She looked at the autumn landscape, heard the rumble of a wagon on the bridge, and the rush of the river.

Leaning her head against the sun-warmed door, she closed her eyes. "God bless Aunt Miranda," she whispered. "God bless the brick house that was. God bless the brick house that is to be!"